3-20-14

*The Best Japanese
Science Fiction Stories*

THE BEST JAPANESE SCIENCE FICTION STORIES

Edited by
JOHN L. APOSTOLOU
and
MARTIN H. GREENBERG

Consulting Editors:
Grania Davis *and* Judith Merril

DEMBNER BOOKS • New York

DEMBNER BOOKS
Published by Red Dembner Enterprises Corp.,
80 Eighth Avenue, New York, N.Y. 10011

Distributed by W. W. Norton & Company, Inc.,
500 Fifth Avenue, New York, N.Y. 10110

Library of Congress Cataloging in Publication Data

The Best Japanese science fiction stories / edited by John L.
  Apostolou and Martin H. Greenberg.
    p. cm.
  ISBN 0-942637-06-2 : $16.95
    1. Science fiction, Japanese—Translations into English.
2. Science fiction, English—Translations from Japanese.
I. Apostolou, John L. II. Greenberg, Martin Harry.
  PL782.E8B4 1989
895.6′30876′08—dc19   88-9577
                                          CIP

Design by Antler & Baldwin, Inc.

*Acknowledgments, permissions and additional
copyright material to be found on page vi.*

To the *Honyaku Benkyokai*
the group of translators
whose special contribution to this book
is gratefully acknowledged.

CONTENTS

FOREWORD

Godzilla and the other wonderful, bizarre super-heroes and monsters, represent the limited image that many people have of Japanese science fiction—but in Japan these creatures are intended for children. Japan's highly imaginative SF and fantasy literature come from an ancient tradition of legends and myths. Yet they are not well known in America, because so little has been translated and published in English. This collection presents Japan's brightest, weirdest, and best speculative fiction, gathered and polished over a number of years by a number of talented translators.

Consider the difficulties of translating science fiction from Japanese to English. The complex nuances of language and culture are often very subtle, and Japanese uses three interchangeable alphabets! How many people are fluent in both languages, familiar with the SF genre, and able to capture the "soul" of a story? Of course the Japanese translators have similar complaints about English, as they struggle with our slang-laden prose. That's why Japanese and English-speaking translators sometimes work together in teams to create a "group-mind" with the author.

I came to know these translators very well, during the two years I lived in a suburb of neon-lit Tokyo. I first visited Japan as a tourist in 1972. Judith Merril, the trail-blazing author and anthologist, was already working with the translators group on many of the stories that appear in this book. I recall intense discussions of the hidden meanings of words like *love*. The work proceeded slowly, word by word, and by the time Judy Merril left Japan, many outstanding stories had been translated.

But more stories were needed to fill an anthology. I returned to live in Japan in 1979. The translators group, known as *Honyaku Benkyokai*, greeted me warmly. "We are crazy alcoholics and workaholics!" crowed the brilliant SF author, Tetsu Yano, who is one of the patriarchs of the group, and whose haunting novella *The Legend of the Paper Spaceship* (superbly translated by Gene Van Troyer) appears in this book. Yano-san spoke the truth. The group worked and partied at a fast-forward Tokyo pace, with a keen sense of fun and creative energy. The translators weekends became the highlights of my life in Japan.

Every month we would meet at a Tokyo train station

on Saturday afternoon, and travel together to some scenic place—for autumn leaf viewing on the slopes of Mt. Fuji, or iris viewing in the springtime, or perhaps to a hot-spring resort or a publisher's seaside villa. We would stay in charming Japanese inns, feast on banquets of local specialities—and talk and drink, laugh and talk far into the night. In the mornings over our artfully arranged Japanese breakfast trays, we would have serious discussions of hangovers. The weekend would end with Sunday sightseeing, more talk and laughter, and the long train ride home.

But we worked hard. Translations of English-language SF are popular in Japan, and the translators must meet strict deadlines. My husband, Dr. Stephen Davis, and I would try to explain complicated English phrases like, "Keep the X in Xmas . . ." I would buttonhole and cajole the group into helping me translate some of the Japanese stories that appear in this anthology. After one especially difficult session, someone in the group exclaimed, "You and Judy Merril are a pair of demon-mothers!" The work was wonderfully exciting. It was a global-village meeting of cultures. My husband and I quickly became part of this Japanese group-mind, and developed a keen appreciation of their wry and dry wit (and their fine dry sake).

By the time I left Japan, in 1980, there were enough _ichiban_ (first-rate) translated stories to fill an anthology— but we had no publisher. "Science fiction readers aren't interested in Japan," claimed the American editors (who clearly had their pre-cog antennae turned off). The anthology project languished, though new stories were translated, and many were published and acclaimed individually.

Then gradually Americans realized that the Japanese are already living in a version of the _future_—with its overcrowding, micro-electronic gadgets, polluted environment, and efficient group-minds. The problems—and solutions—of the future are happening in Japan right *now*. Japanese science fiction gives us an insight into that future—often a shocking, yet witty and satiric insight.

Interest in Japanese culture grew as rapidly as the value of the yen in the late 1980s. It was time to correct the trade imbalance in science fiction. The noted anthologist, Martin Greenberg, and John Apostolou, who is keenly interested in Japanese literature, were finally able to arrange publication with Dembner Books. I am proud to be part of both the translation group-mind and the editorial group-mind.

Grania Davis, Consulting Editor
San Rafael, California

INTRODUCTION

For many Americans the words "Japanese science fiction" conjure up images of a gigantic monster destroying parts of downtown Tokyo, but this is a gross misconception. Japanese SF is a vital and varied genre, worthy of serious consideration.

During the 1950s and '60s, when the early Godzilla films were being produced, another development was taking place in Japan: the emergence of a group of talented

SF writers. Although little known outside Japan, they have written short stories and novels of quality and even brilliance. It is hoped that this anthology, the *first* anthology of Japanese SF in English, will introduce these authors to a new audience and gain for them the recognition in the West that they deserve.

Science fiction has been published in Japan for over a hundred years, the earliest examples being translations of novels by Jules Verne. SF works by Japanese authors began to appear in print at about the turn of the century. Shunro Oshikawa (1877–1914) and Juzo Unno (1897–1949) were prominent writers in the early days of Japanese SF. Inspired by Verne and H.G. Wells, they often wrote novels combining military adventures with science, such as Oshikawa's *The Undersea Warship* (1900) and Unno's *The Floating Airfield* (1938).

In the decades prior to World War II, Japanese SF stories were usually imitations of Western models, emphasizing gadgetry and the technological marvels of the future. Generally speaking, Japanese critics looked upon science fiction as a subliterary form and, for some odd reason, placed it within the mystery genre.

When American forces occupied Japan after the war, many GIs brought with them SF magazines and paperbacks, items that would later be found in the used book stores of Tokyo and other major cities. Exposure to this material led to a revival of science fiction in Japan, and soon translations of Ray Bradbury and Isaac Asimov were on the best-seller lists. The popularity of the genre, both in print and in visual media, has continued to the present day.

In 1957, two important events in the development of Japanese SF took place. The now-legendary fanzine *Uchujin* (*Cosmic Dust*) was founded, and Hayakawa Shobo began publishing its long and successful series of SF books. In

1960, Hayakawa Shobo published the first issue of *SF Magazine*, the leading professional SF periodical in Japan today. Most important Japanese SF writers had their first stories appear in *Uchujin* and were later published in *SF Magazine*.

Fan activity began in the late 1950s. SF clubs were formed and many of them published fanzines similar to *Uchujin*. A tradition of annual SF conventions started in 1962, with the first such event staged in Tokyo. Takumi Shibano, the editor of *Uchujin*, and author Tetsu Yano were major names in the early years of Japanese SF fandom, and they are still involved in fan activities today.

Despite the increase in SF publications and the growth of SF fandom, most of the science fiction published in Japan in the 1960s were translations of stories and novels written in English. But a new wave of Japanese SF writers had arrived on the scene. Men of originality and talent, they were not content to imitate the work of American and British authors. This anthology is comprised of short stories by these writers and those who followed in their footsteps.

The ten authors represented in this book were born in the 1920s and '30s. The senior member of the group is Tetsu Yano, born in 1923; the youngest is Tensei Kono, born in 1935. This means they all lived through World War II and the occupation years, and references to that difficult period can be found in their work.

The three major figures in this group, sometimes called "the big three" of Japanese SF are Ryo Hanmura, Shinichi Hoshi, and Sakyo Komatsu. Hanmura's prodigious literary output includes historical novels as well as science fiction. His most popular SF books are part of a continuing series in which he narrates a fictitious history of ancient Japan. His stories sometimes contain elements of mysticism and the occult.

One of Japan's most popular and prolific authors, Shinichi Hoshi has written over one thousand short stories. Hoshi writes in a simple style, producing stories that are brief (many are short shorts) and often humorous. Some of his stories could be classified as works of fantasy or mystery fiction.

Japan's most successful SF writer, Sakyo Komatsu also writes scientific nonfiction. He is best known as the author of the runaway best-seller *Nippon Chimbotsu* (1973), translated into English as *Japan Sinks* (1976), a novel set in the near future when the entire island chain of Japan is in danger of submersion. Komatsu concentrates on the efforts of scientists and government officials to save the Japanese people and their culture from destruction.

Two of the authors in this book, Kobo Abe and Morio Kita, are mainstream fiction writers who occasionally produce science fiction. A world-famous author of Kafkaesque prose, Abe has had seven novels translated into English. The best known of these is *The Woman in the Dunes* (1964). Morio Kita has two historical novels in English (actually a long novel published in two parts), *The House of Nire* (1984) and *The Fall of the House of Nire* (1985).

The five remaining authors—Takashi Ishikawa, Tensei Kono, Taku Mayumura, Yasutaka Tsutsui, and Tetsu Yano—are all prominent SF writers. Ishikawa is also Japan's leading SF critic, and Yano, the patriarch of Japanese SF, is active as a translator of American and British SF into Japanese.

Although the works of these writers are in many respects similar to science fiction produced in the West, Japanese SF is evolving its own characteristics. Surprisingly few Japanese SF writers are genuinely interested in science or technological advances. The term "speculative fiction" seems a more accurate label for their work than science fiction.

The future holds no great fascination for most of Japan's SF writers; instead, they use the genre to examine the past and the present, attempting to understand their rapidly changing society. In his excellent piece on Japanese SF in the third edition of the reference book *Anatomy of Wonder* (1987), David Lewis says: "Japanese SF writers share the national preoccupation with the past; their work does not seek a path to the future so much as the hidden trail to today."

In roughly one hundred years, Japan has developed from a nation with a nearly feudal culture to a modern economic giant. Despite the boom of recent years, the Japanese people retain a deeply rooted anxiety growing out of the fact the country has so few natural resources. It is not surprising that many Japanese SF writers should choose to explore the social implications of change, producing what could be called parables or cautionary tales. In these works, direct and indirect references are made to historical periods and events—the era of militarism and thought control in the 1930s and '40s, World War II, the atomic bombings of Hiroshima and Nagasaki. Questions are raised about the impact of rapid modernization, the pollution of the environment, the dangers of insular thinking, and the myth of racial superiority.

But Japanese SF is not always as serious as this discussion might indicate. Even when dealing with weighty subjects, the best Japanese SF, such as the stories selected for this anthology, is often leavened with humor or poetic feeling.

Although Japanese SF films have been exhibited in theaters around the world, the works of Japan's SF writers are little known outside that country. Only a small number of translations of Japanese SF are available in English.

The first Japanese SF novel to be translated into English was *Inter Ice Age 4* (1970) by Kobo Abe. As with *Japan Sinks*, Abe's novel concerns the submersion of land masses; but, in this case, the entire world is in danger, not just the islands of Japan. Central to the plot are the activities of a secret organization that is transforming terrestrial mammals, including humans, into acquatic creatures which would be able to survive the flood.

The first Japanese SF short story to appear in English was "Bokko-chan" by Shinichi Hoshi in the June 1963 issue of *The Magazine of Fantasy and Science Fiction*. The first single-author collection of Japanese SF short stories was Hoshi's *The Spiteful Planet and Other Stories* (1978). The first anthology of Japanese SF stories—you hold in your hands. Most of the stories in this book were translated in a collaborative effort of several years' duration, involving Grania Davis, Judith Merril, and members of a group of translators, the *Honyaku Benkyokai*.

The Kodansha English Library, a paperback series of Japanese popular fiction in English translation, was launched in 1984. Published primarily for young Japanese students of English, this ongoing series includes SF story collections by Hoshi and Yasutaka Tsutsui, and SF novels by Haruka Takachiho and Motoko Arai, one of the few female SF writers in Japan. Although not readily available in the United States, the Kodansha English Library, a commendable venture, is certainly worthy of mention.

The editors hope this anthology will stimulate interest in Japanese SF, perhaps resulting in some critical work on the subject and in the production of more translations.

Since the Japanese are great believers in group effort, it is appropriate that this book be the result of teamwork. In addition to the stalwart efforts of my collaborator Martin

Greenberg, I must acknowledge the valuable contributions made by consulting editors Grania Davis and Judith Merril, the ten authors of the selected stories, the fifteen translators (including Davis, Merril, and author Tetsu Yano), and Violet Margosian, who helped prepare the manuscript. A most sincere *arigato* to you all.

John L. Apostolou
Los Angeles
October 1988

KOBO ABE

THE FLOOD

Translated by Lane Dunlop

Humankind is threatened by a new disease—liquefaction.

A certain poor but honest philosopher, to study the laws of the universe, took a telescope up to the roof of his tenement and pursued the movements of the heavenly bodies. As always, he seemed unable to discover more than a few meaningless shooting stars and the stars in their usual positions. It was not that he was bored or anything, but he happened to turn his telescope casually on the earth. An upsidedown road dangled in front of his nose. A similarly inverted worker appeared, walking backwards along the road. Righting these images in his head, and returning them to their usual relationship, the philosopher adjusted the lens and followed the worker's movements. Under the wide-bore lens, the interior of the worker's little head was transparent. The reason was that the worker, on his way back from the night shift at the factory, had nothing in his head but fatigue.

However, the persevering philosopher, not turning the lens aside because of that, continued to follow the worker's progress. the philosopher's patience was soon rewarded. Suddenly, the following changes took place in the worker.

The outline of the worker's body unexpectedly grew blurred. Melting from the feet up, the figure knelt slimily and dissolved. Only the clothes, cap, and shoes remained, in a mass of fleshy liquid. Finally, completely fluid, it spread out flat on the ground.

The liquefied worker quietly began to flow toward lower ground. He flowed into a pothole. Then he crawled out of it. This movement of the liquid worker, in defiance of the laws of hydrodynamics, amazed the philosopher so much that he almost dropped the telescope. Flowing onward, the worker, when he came up against a roadside fence, crawled up it just like a snail gliding on its membrane, and disappeared from view over the fence. The philosopher, taking his eye from the telescope, heaved a deep sigh. The next day, he announced to the world the coming of a great flood.

Actually, everywhere in the world, the liquefaction of workers and poor people had begun. Particularly remarkable were the group liquefactions. In a large factory, the machinery would suddenly stop. The workers, deliquescing all at once, would form a single mass of liquid that flowed in a stream under the door or, crawling up the wall, flowed out the window. Sometimes the process was reversed: after the workers had turned into liquid, only the machinery, in the deserted factory, would senselessly continue running and in the end break down, In addition, breakouts from prisons due to the mass liquefaction of the prisoners and small floods caused by the liquefaction of whole populations of farm villages were reported one after another in the newspapers.

The liquefaction of human beings, not limited to this kind of phenomenal abnormality, occasioned confusion in a variety of ways. Perfect crimes owing to the liquefaction of the criminal increased dramatically. Law and order were threatened. The police, secretly mobilizing the physicists, began an investigation of the properties of this water. But the liquid, completely ignoring the scientific laws of fluids, merely plunged the physicists into ludicrous confusion. Although to the touch it was in no way different from an ordinary water, at times it displayed a strong surface tension like mercury and could retain its shape like amoebae, so that not only could it crawl, as indicated before, from a low to a higher place, but after blending perfectly with its fellow liquefied people and other natural liquids, at some impulse or other it could also separate itself into its original volume. Again, conversely, it sometimes displayed a weak surface tension like that of alcohol. At such times, it had an extraordinary power of permeation vis-à-vis all solids. E.g., at times, probably in relation to differences in its use, with the same kind of paper it could either have absolutely no effect or could dissolve it chemically.

The liquefied human beings were also able to freeze or evaporate. Their freezing and evaporation points were various. Sleighs running over thick ice would be swallowed up horse and all by the suddenly melted ice; front-runners in skating contests would abruptly vanish. Again, swimming pools would suddenly freeze in midsummer, sealing up girls who'd been swimming in them in frozen poses in the ice. The liquid human beings crawled up mountains, mixed with rivers, crossed oceans, evaporated into clouds and fell as rain, so that they spread all over the world. One could never tell what kind of thing was going to happen when and where. Chemistry experiments became well-nigh impossible. The boilers of steam engines, because of an admixture of liquid people, became completely unserviceable. No matter how much they were stoked, no pressure built up. Or all of a sudden the liquid people would violently expand and explode the boiler. Fish and plants that had a vital relationship to water were in a state of chaos beyond description. In every field of biology, transformations were difficult to calculate, and destructions, had begun. Apples rolled around warbling snatches of melody; rice stalks burst with a noise like firecrackers. Especially serious were the effects on human beings who had not yet deliquesced, and in particular on rich people.

One morning, the owner of a big factory drowned in a cup of coffee as soon as he put his lips to the cup. Another industrialist drowned in a glass of whiskey. An extreme example was a drowning in a single drop of eyewash. These seem like things scarcely to be believed, but they all happened.

As these facts were reported, many rich people contracted hydrophobia in the true sense of the word. A certain high government official made the following confession: "When I'm about to drink, I look at the water in the glass and already it does not seem like water to me. In short, it is a liquidized mineral, a harmful substance that is impossible to digest. If I took a mouthful, I am positive I would immediately get sick. I'm instantly invaded by tragic fears."

Even if dysphagia were not present, this was plainly hydrophobia. Everywhere, there were instances of old ladies who fainted away at the mere sight of water. Yet antirabies vaccine did no good whatsoever.

By now, from one end of the world to the other, invisible voices were mingling in a chorus crying doom by a great flood. But the newspapers, at first publishing the following reasons, strenuously denied those rumors:

a) This year's rainfall, both regional and global, is below the annual average.

b) All rivers reported to have flooded have not exceeded the seasonal variation for a normal year.

c) No meteorological or geological abnormalities have been observed.

These were the facts. But it was also a fact that the flood had already started. This contradiction caused general social unrest. It was already clear to everyone that this was no ordinary flood. Presently even the newspapers were forced to acknowledge the reality of the flood. But in their usual optimistic tone, they reiterated that this was due to some cosmic accident, was no more than temporary, and would soon end of its own accord. However, the flood, spreading daily, engulfed many villages and towns, many flatlands and low hills were submerged by the liquid people, and the people of status, the people of wealth, began a competitive stampede for refuge in the upland and mountain districts. Although realizing that that kind of thing was useless against the liquid people who climbed even walls, they were unable to think of anything else to do.

Finally, even the presidents and prime ministers admitted the urgency of the situation. Proclamations were issued, saying that in order to save humanity from extinction in this flood it was necessary to mobilize all spiritual and material resources and expedite the building of great dams and dikes. Tens of thousands of workers, for that purpose, were rounded up for compulsory labor. Whereupon the newspapers also, suddenly changing their attitude, chimed in with the proclamations and praised their high morality and sense of public duty. But just about everybody, including the presidents and prime ministers, knew that those proclamations were nothing more than proclamations for the sake of proclamations. Dikes and such, against the liquid people, being no more than Newtonian dynamics against quantum dynamics, were completely ineffectual. Not only that, but the workers constructing the dikes were rapidly turning into liquid this side of the dikes. The "personal items" pages of the newspapers were awash with notices of missing persons. But, true to character, the newspapers dealt with such disappearances simply as effects rather than causes of the flood. In regard to the contradictory nature of the flood and its essential cause, they maintained a resolute silence, refusing even to mention the subject.

At this time, there was a scientist who proposed that the liquid that had covered the earth be volatilized by means of nuclear energy. The governments, speedily indicating their approval, pledged their full-scale assistance. But when they tried to begin, what became clear, rather than various difficulties, was the impossibility of the project. Because of the liquefaction of human beings, which was accelerating at geometrical progression, there were not enough workers for adequate replacements. Also, liquefaction was already occurring among the scientists. Furthermore, the parts factories were steadily being destroyed and engulfed by the waters. Harassed by problems of reorganization and reconstruction, governments could not predict when the production of vital nuclear equipment would begin.

Unrest and distress swept the world. People were turning into mummies from dehydration, emitting gasping, rattling noises each time they breathed.

There was just one person who was calm and happy. This was the optimistic and wily Noah. Noah, from his experience with the previous flood, without getting agitated or panicky, diligently worked on his ark. When he thought that the future of the human race was being entrusted to him and his family alone, he was even able to steep himself in a religious exaltation.

Presently, when the flood approached his house, Noah, accompanied by his family and domestic animals, boarded the ark. Immediately, the liquid people started to crawl up the sides of the boat. Noah berated them in a loud voice.

"Hey! Whose boat do you think this is? I am Noah. This is Noah's Ark. Make no mistake about it. Go on, get out of here!"

But to think that the liquid, which was no longer human, could understand his words was clearly a hasty conclusion and a miscalculation. For liquid, there are only concerns of liquid. The next minute, the ark filled up with liquid and the living creatures drowned. The derelict ark drifted at the mercy of the wind.

In this manner, humanity perished in the Second Flood. But, if you could have looked at the street corners and under the trees of the villages at the bottom of the now-peaceful waters, you would have seen a glittering substance starting to crystallize. Probably around the invisible core of the supersaturated liquid people.

RYO HANMURA

CARDBOARD BOX

Translated by David Lewis

Contemplated in allegory is the fate of ordinary working people.

Suddenly, I perceived myself.

If that's what you call birth, it was pretty disappointing. Then my body, bent and folded flat, was quickly unfolded, and in the next instant I was overturned and enraptured with the sensation of my bottom being fitted together and closed.

To tell the truth, I came into the world without having any idea of what was happening to me.

Even so, I still remember how strong and dependable I felt myself to be when that wide tape, sucking tight against my skin was criss-crossed across my bottom. But that was only for the shortest of moments. Again I was spun round, and turned right side up. When I think back on it, I realize that by then I was already on the conveyor belt, but at the time I was completely absorbed in sensing the white fluorescent light that filled my surroundings, and I didn't even notice that I was moving, swaying as I went.

My comrades . . . perhaps I should say my brothers? In any case, it was when we were riding that belt conveyor that I first realized that they and I were separate entities. They were swaying in front of me and behind me, and I thought to myself that I, too, was swaying just like them.

They had the same markings on their bodies as I had on mine. We were exactly the same size. In fact, it was at that time that I first realized I had markings on my own body as well.

I was feeling a bit forlorn. I had just been born and didn't understand things clearly, but I couldn't help feeling that I wasn't closely attached to them.

I was born and, thus separated from my brothers, began to exist. Perhaps I felt forlorn because I wasn't used to an independent existence.

I spoke to the comrade closest to me to drive away the loneliness.

"I wonder why we're swaying?"

My comrades, well-mannered, were all queued up in a line, swaying from side to side. The one I spoke to was directly in front of me in the queue.

"How should I know?" he answered.

"We're moving. We're being transported someplace," said the one behind me.

"I wonder where we're going?"

"How should I know?" he answered. He spoke exactly like the one in front of me.

"In any case, we're going to be filled. Isn't that good enough?"

The comrade behind me was suddenly overjoyed.

"We'll be filled! Hey, everybody! From now on we're going to be filled!"

Pleasure spread through all my queued-up comrades when he cried out.

"We'll be filled! We'll be filled! We'll all be filled!"

A chorus began, and before I knew it I, too, had joined in. "It's good to be alive," I thought. In a few moments I'd be filled. This body of mine would be filled completely. that was my vindication for living. That was my purpose in life.

My body shook, not just because of the conveyor belt, but with joy. The expectation that in a moment I would be filled left me on Cloud Nine. But suddenly I heard a thin, whooshing sound, and we were given an even more violent shaking. I had a sense of falling forward, and was on the verge of tumbling dangerously from the conveyor belt.

"What happened?" asked a worried voice from behind. "We're not going anywhere."

"Good Lord! Surely they're not going to tell us to stay as we are! This isn't funny. Hurry up and fill us!"

Unease spread to everybody the moment the conveyor belt stopped. Of course I also waited nervously for the movement to resume. If I had to spend my whole life like this with an empty body . . . Just thinking of it made me cry out, abandoning all propriety.

"Move! Don't leave us like this!"

That stoppage was agony. Not only had we yet to be filled, we still didn't have anything at all in our bodies.

How long did that uneasy time continue? I have a feeling it was a very long time. By the time the conveyor began, with a thudding impact, to move again, we were at our wits' end, not even caring if we weren't filled, just so long as something, anything was put into our bodies.

"Anything'll do; I want something put in fast!" Writhing with base desires, I was transported to the end of the conveyor belt before I knew it.

Ecstasy came suddenly.

A round, flexible something rushed into a corner of my square body.

Aaah . . . I shivered.

For the first time since my birth I was numb with the pleasure driven into my body. The round, pliable objects lithely and accurately began to fill me. My pleasure mounted as the accumulated weight of the objects increased. I will never forget the pleasure of that moment, mounting higher and higher, leaving me no time even to breathe. My bottom was buried without a gap, and the objects climbed steadily higher and higher.

Then at last I was full. I had been completely filled!

Even then my body was being moved. When I was completely full and quivering with the pleasure of it, the top of my body was suddenly bent and folded again, and that tape that sucked tight against my skin sealed my body tight.

I felt myself powerful with a strength ten times that I had felt before. My adequately filled self slid down an incline, was pulled around, heaved and piled, but even that violence was not painful, as though somewhere within it was a gentle consideration.

I came to rest. No sooner had I come to rest than the weight of my comrades came down on top of me. I myself was positioned on top of more of my comrades. In the end, in front, in back, to right and left, I was tight against the bodies of my comrades, filled and quivering with joy.

"It's wonderful! I'm completely full!"

That shout could be heard from somewhere among my piled-up companions. I, too, was lucky like the owner of that voice. I felt I had been born for pleasure.

It appeared that, still piled up, we had begun to move again. But this time it was in darkness. In the midst of ceaseless small vibrations and occasional leisurely swaying, I felt myself to be completely satisfied.

However, from far away towards the edge of our pile, a voice started up, filled with sarcasm.

"You all seem pretty smug, don't you now."

The voice was hoarse as though tired.

"Well, it's something to be satisfied about. But it's not going to last for long."

"Who's talking like that?" asked one of my comrades cheerily.

"Hey, heh," returned the sarcastic hoarse voice. "Right now we're being taken to town in a truck. When we get there, you'll all have your lids cut open, and you'll have to cough up all those things you've got in you bodies."

"Liar! Who could think of emptying us so soon, now that we've finally been filled . . ."

"You're still a lot of babies," ridiculed Hoarse Voice. "First off, you probably don't even know what you've got in your bodies."

"I don't know," admitted another voice from the back. "What are those round things, tell us!"

"Oh, I'll tell you all right," said Hoarse Voice. "They're tangerines. The things you got stuffed in your bodies are tangerines. When tangerines get to town they're divided up and sent to stores, piled up and sold. That's why you're all going to get your lids cut open and be emptied."

We, the load of a truck, were returned to silence.

"That's okay. Maybe it can't be helped," said one of my companions who seemed to be near Hoarse Voice. "We're filled with tangerines. No doubt it's true. Tangerines are transported to town and sold in stores. Probably that's true, too. That's why we've been filled with tangerines and are being taken to town. And then, probably, when we reach the town, our lids will be cut and we'll cough up our tangerines—"

A voice that was not quite a shriek and not quite a sigh filled the truck.

"But that's not the end, right? We're a species born to have our bodies filled!"

"With something more than air, that is," said Hoarse Voice nastily.

"That's right," continued the second voice with strong self control, not rising to Hoarse Voice's challenge. "We are boxes. Cardboard boxes. We can do more than just hold tangerines. Even after we've had our tangerines taken out we can still hold other things."

"That's right, all right," laughed Hoarse Voice. "In my body right now there's a cotton jacket and a dirty towel and a lunch box and a pair of old shoes. They belong to the driver of this truck. But that's not what it was like before.

"I was a box full of writing materials. Writing materials like kids use at school. Writing materials, each bugger wrapped up proper, filling me to the brim. I was filled! Even I wasn't like this in the beginning."

For some reason Hoarse Voice began to get angry.

"You can put anything in a box. But even so, you guys, the world is like that. You were made to put tangerines in. They stuff tangerines into your bodies, and after they've all been taken out, not one left behind, nobody cares what'll happen to you."

"No!!"

"It's true! No mistake about it. After the tangerines are gone you guys are just empty boxes. Bothersome, troublesome empty cardboard boxes. Even the guys who made you never thought about what happens after that."

"That's terrible . . ." somebody began to cry. "You mean when these tangerines reach their destination, that's the end?"

Hoarse Voice began to laugh crazily.

"That's right! That's right! You all get the can!"

"What happens then?"

"If your luck's bad, you'll be burned right off and turned into ash. If it goes like usual, you'll have your bottom tape yanked off. You'll be folded up flat, piled and left somewhere. In a while you'll be gathered together and taken away someplace, and that's the end of it."

"After I've been emptied of tangerines, my body will never be filled again?"

"After that, it's fate. It's up to fate. If your luck's good they may put in something else. Like me, an oily cotton jacket, dirty towels, old shoes . . ."

"Anything's fine. I want to be filled! I want to live!"

"It's better to resign yourself. A box you put tangerines in is a tangerine box. A tangerine box with its tangerines gone is garbage. Then you guys, you've got 'tangerine box' written all over you. Even if you get, like, bundles of money stuffed into you, a tangerine box is still a tangerine box."

"On that body of yours . . ." the comrade right next to Hoarse Voice seemed to be looking over his companion's body. "You've got 'pencil box' written on you, don't you. Were you a box for putting pencils in?"

Hoarse Voice laughed crazily again.

"I'm a box for putting pencil boxes in! I told you.

There's good luck and bad luck. I'm not lucky, not me. In this cardboard box called me, pencil boxes like elementary school kids use. . . . You get that? Even a pencil box is a box!"

Hoarse Voice had begun to cry.

"A box for putting boxes in! I was a box for putting boxes in! There's nothing inside a pencil box before it's sold. It's an empty box! And those were stuffed into me. . . .

"Can you understand that feeling? Filled in form only. It's not like you've really been filled. You're filled with empty boxes! You guys here worrying about what happens after you get to town and have your tangerines taken out, that's a luxury! Aren't you filled and happy enough to shiver!"

"Hey, Mr. Pencil Box, don't cry."

"I'm not a pencil box! I'm a box for pencil boxes!"

"But even after you were emptied aren't you still alive? Cheer up!"

My comrades all joined in, trying to encourage the old cardboard box with the hoarse voice. But even then we were approaching the town that was to be our final destination.

Lowered from the truck, we were scattered far and wide under the sun. It was a bustling vegetable and fruit market, and there I had no choice but to observe a most blood-curdling scene.

Right next to where I and two or three of my comrades had been placed together in a clump a big bonfire was blazing. People gathered around that fire, rubbing their hands together coldly. Now and then they fed the fire scraps of wood, and empty cardboard boxes from among my comrades.

I had to sit there and stare at what my end would be.

A sense of helplessness welled up within me. My sole salvation were the tangerines still stuffed within my body.

However, as I gazed upon my comrades burning up one after the other, I suddenly awoke to the truth that I was not really full. Considerable gaps remained between the round tangerines. Every time I thought of the dark road ahead, my heart grew wilder with the thought that my present half-filled state was not enough.

'I want to be filled more! I want this body filled until not a single gap remains!'

Consumed with lust, I forgot myself. "Put more in! Even fuller!" I screamed, even though I was already tightly closed with tape.

"Hey! Calm down!" My comrades rebuked me, unable to contain themselves, but I continued to scream.

"Put more in! Even fuller!"

For a tangerine box, I enjoyed the greatest of luck. Right after being transported from the market to the town's fruit store, the other two boxes with me were opened and the tangerines inside them were piled up in front of the store by shop attendants. But I was placed, untouched, in the back of the store. Two, three days passed, but I stayed put on the concrete floor. Until the second day I had my two empty comrades beside me, but on the third day they were folded up roughly by the shopkeeper and taken away.

Just before being folded, one of them shouted in my direction.

"Farewell! It was an empty life!"

I tried to say something in return, but he had already ceased to exist as a box.

A box is for putting things in. It is in having things put into them that boxes find pleasure in life. When things are packed in lightly, a box's body can shiver with insurmountable gratification.

Yet people make boxes just to put tangerines in, and once that duty is finished, even if a box can still be used, they abandon it without a care. I have no way of knowing what happened to my comrades forsaken in this way, but no doubt every one of them had their lives as boxes closed out.

Fortunately for me, I was chanced upon by a customer who wanted to buy a whole box of tangerines and was taken to his house by one of the fruit store attendants. There I was pushed onto a warm dark shelf in the kitchen and had the tangerines inside me taken out little by little.

Only at that time was I unable to complain that I was empty, that I was not filled. Instead, I prayed desperately that I could buy even a little more time before the last tangerine was taken away.

But that did not take long. My emptied self was dragged out to a bright place and was cast away. Then, in a short while, people began, little by little, to fill me again.

Beer bottle caps and thick plastic bags, padding used for packing, all kinds of nonflammable garbage was tossed inside me.

Even with that, I was satisfied. It doesn't matter what's inside. Just so long as its body is filled, a box is satisfied.

And at last, I was filled. It was the second climax of my life. Filled with nonflammable garbage, I was left alone for more than half a year.

My good luck continued. One day, my nonflammable friends quickly left my body. By all rights, my own life should have ended there as well, but for some reason only my contents were thrown away and I was left in the street outside the house. There the children came, one getting inside my body and two others pushing and pulling the two of us around. I was worn threadbare on the concrete road, but I was enraptured with being filled by human children.

The children took the game to heart. They carried me to a nearby park with a pond, and played there over and over again every day. In just a few days I was worn out, but I was still alive. Perhaps I was able to last longer because I had the dirt of the path beneath me instead of concrete.

But as far as having anything put into me again, it was hopeless. My corners were split. I was full of holes. Never again would I be able to perform my role as a box.

Then the children tired of their game with me. One windy night I was blown over by a gust, and drew closer to the pond.

To a cardboard box, water is an object of terror. The wind maliciously pushed me toward the water's edge.

"This is the end. . . ."

I resigned myself to my fate. The wind blew stronger, and at last I was blown over and fell onto the water. Fallen, but still floating. I was blown by the wind like a sailing ship, and moved toward the center of the pond.

A cardboard box fears the water. And that water soaked steadily into my body. I began to sink, unable to move even when blown by the wind. The water infiltrated me, making my body ridiculously heavy.

Sinking. I was sinking.

The park where I had passed the hours playing with the children was lost to my sight. The sky, the wind, both passed from my consciousness.

"Here my life has come to an end:" so thinking, I gave myself up. Slowly, slowly, I sank toward the bottom of the pond.

Aaah . . . What ecstacy . . .

I was enraptured. I was filled! For the first time in my life I was completely filled! The water, with perfect, even density, was filling my body!

It was an ecstacy like melting. Indeed, my body would

no doubt dissolve in the water. Yet wasn't that the same as dissolving in the ecstacy of being filled?

As I quietly submerged, my body swamped with water, I was numb with joy.

"It no longer matters if I die," I whispered. Could there ever have been another cardboard box so perfectly filled? Could there ever have been another cardboard box who ended his life in such ecstacy. . . .

I no longer have need for the concept of time. I, adequately filled at last and gently dissolving away, am now in the midst of joy.

RYO HANMURA

TANSU

*Translated by Shimizu Hitomi, Joel Dames,
Stephen Davis, and Grania Davis*

*A strange story concerning an old
wooden chest.*

"Well now, my oldest son is an unsociable son man,"
said the old woman in her rough country dialect, "so even
if he's invited to gatherings like this he keeps quiet. But
that doesn't mean he don't like you, so please don't mind
him.

"You see, his brothers all left—went into the Self-
Defense Force. Noto here might sound like a pretty nice
place because lots of tourists come visiting from Tokyo or

Osaka, but we can't get nothing. Noto is near the sea, and we throw out our nets in spots. But catching fish is a gamble. When summer comes, we can't catch many fish.

"I reckon in the old days, every house around here had them sliding, painted *fusama* closet doors and heavy lacquered and carved woodwork. They took plenty time to build. They seem pretty strange to folks from Shichosaburo's. It's dark at night in these houses, even if you light the lamps. There's too many rooms, and unless we have something like a big funeral gathering, there's rooms we don't use for months. So I suppose it's natural if you're scared to sleep by yourself.

"If you can't get to sleep, I can tell you something kind of strange," continued the old woman in her soft rural drawl. "Well, I'm sorry I'm not a good story-teller like a priest, who can drone on until you're sound asleep. I'm just an old woman and I only know some old stories—but this one is pretty strange.

"Truth is, this story happened right in this house. My granny told me about it, but I'm not sure when it happened. Sometime in the past, when the head of this house was a fisherman called Ichisuke.

"When Ichisuke was in his prime working years, his own father and mother were still healthy; and he had a wife and eight children, ranging from age sixteen to a three-year-old boy.

"In those days, and those days aren't so long past, everyone had plenty children. I don't know what they do nowadays. Not so many kids—instead they live with their TV and refrigerator.

"But I reckon it's better nowadays, much better. The kids had them boils or runny eyes in the old days. And the old folks' backs were soon bent. Ichisuke's parents were probably bent over when they grew old.

"Ichisuke went to the beach early every morning and sailed offshore on his boat. I suppose working the paddy fields and farm was his wife's job; and the old people and older children helped her. Hear tell they all lived happily together.

"But according to the story, one day the three-year-old started acting mighty strange. At night he didn't sleep at all. He got up onto a big old *tansu* chest every night, and just sat there like this till dawn.

"Now Ichisuke didn't know about it at first. When he finally found out, a long time had passed.

"I reckon he was pretty surprised, and went and yelled at his wife, 'Why do you let him behave so strange? I'll spank him if you don't keep him in his bedroom from now on!'

"But his wife saw the boy sitting on the *tansu* again that night, and she didn't say nothing.

"Well Ichisuke was fuming mad. He pulled the boy off the *tansu* chest and hit him.

"Now you understand that the wife and kids were usually very docile and obeyed Ichisuke. But this here seemed different. Eveyone ignored the problem and wouldn't talk to Ichisuke about it, even though he asked them again and again. They let the boy sit on the *tansu* because he wouldn't listen when they told him to stop.

"Well Ichisuke gave in. He figured his son would outgrow such childish behavior, and he left the boy alone.

"Some time after that, I'm not sure when, Ichisuke peeped into the children's bedroom, thinking it was about time that his boy stopped sitting on the *tansu* chest at night.

"Well I mentioned that there were eight children altogether. When he peeped into their rooms, five out of the eight were missing! He found them all in one room, on the same old *tansu* chest, just sitting quietly on their legs with their hands on their knees, exactly like the youngest son!

"He was astonished, as you can imagine. 'What's everyone doing up there?' he yelled.

"But I'm told they didn't seem to hear. They just sat there. He was scared and woke up the rest of the family and made them come into this room.

"It seemed everyone knew about it already. No one was surprised. They all went back to their bedrooms, annoyed that he woke them up over such a thing. Only Ichisuke didn't understand why the children sat on the *tansu*, and when this thing began. Everyone else seemed to know all about it.

"Ichisuke begged his wife, 'Why are they doing such a strange thing? Please, tell me if you know!'

"But I reckon his wife just smiled vaguely and gazed at him, pretending that she didn't understand.

"They say Ichisuke grew very worried. He figured they were sick, and thought it would be horrible if each child caught the disease. He was half right. They were fine physically, even though they spent all night just sitting on the *tansu*—but they were catching it, one after another, just as he feared.

"So then the other three children began to sit up there at night, and even his mother with the bent back—I don't know how she climbed up to such a high place.

"Well finally Ichisuke was scared to stay in the house. Everyone acted the same as usual during the day. But at night they all fell silent and became pale and stiff as dolls, as they sat like this on the old *tansu* chest.

"Hear tell he was so frightened he couldn't sleep—just like you are now my friend.

"But I guess no one can manage without any sleep.

One night when he finally dozed off, he heard a faint sound; *katan, katan, katan, katan* . . . he had heard that sound before.

"'I wonder what's making that noise,' he muttered. It came closer as he strained his ears. *Katan, katan, katan, katan*. . . . The sound came closer and closer.

"Well he turned to his wife who usually slept next to him, wanting to wake her up. She wasn't there. He leaped out of bed, terrified. He ran towards the strange sound, his feet deliberately making heavy slapping sounds, *dota, dota*. . . .

"So then he saw that everyone, his mother and father, wife and children were all working together to bring another old *tansu* chest up the path from the beach, into the house.

"Now Ichisuke couldn't speak, and just watched them bringing it into this back room. The metal handle rings on the old *tansu* made the noise, *katan* . . . *katan*. . . .

"After a while everyone disappeared into the back room, and he couldn't hear those ring sounds anymore. It grew very quiet.

"Fearfully, Ichisuke peeped into the room.

"They say his father and mother, wife and eight children were all there, sitting on both *tansus* with their hands on their laps. They sat still and upright with their eyes wide open.

"I reckon after that night Ichisuke was the only one who slept in his bedroom at night.

"Well I don't know how many nights Ichisuke endured the situation in the house. Finally, one night I hear he got very drunk at his relatives' house, and he decided to escape—anywhere. He ran along the shoreline path with only them same old clothes he was wearing.

"I'm told after he ran away from home, he became a

sailor on a big cargo ship. He didn't come back for several years, but he still sent money to his family. He was a faithful and loyal man.

"Well after some years, his ship happened to sail around to this shore for some reason or another. The boat dropped anchor at a little cape a short distance from here, and stayed there.

"Since this was Ichisuke's home, the place where he was born and raised, he felt very drawn to it. He yearned to go ashore. Though the night was far advanced, he couldn't stay below decks. He just stood leaning against the bow of the ship, staring into the darkness towards his house.

"Well then he heard the sound of a small row boat coming near his ship, and also the soft sound, *katan* . . . *katan* . . . *katan*. . . . It was the sound of the *tansu!* Ichisuke stood there motionless.

"*Katan* . . . *katan* . . . *katan*. . . .

"So then the rowboat pulled up beneath him, and Ichisuke saw that his whole family was in the boat. They all looked up at him imploringly.

"'Father, Father,' they all called to him quietly, 'Father, we want to welcome you home. Please come back. There's nothing to be afraid of. We brought your old *tansu* chest. Please sit on it while we row you back to shore. If your sit on the *tansu* tonight, you'll understand why we do it. Let's live together again. It'll be much nicer than the life of a sailor!' They all called and begged to Ichisuke.

"They say Ichisuke climbed down from the ship that night, and sat on the *tansu* while his family carried him home."

"I think it's a rather strange story, isn't it?" the old woman softly asked her sleepless guest. "I understand why they climbed up on the *tansus* and sat there at night, but I can't explain it properly. I'm not trying to hide anything, I just can't express it in words.

"Actually, there are a lot of old *tansus* in this house by now. I think it's fortunate that you came to visit tonight. Why don't you try to climb up here and sit on the *tansu* yourself. Then maybe you'll understand."

SHINICHI HOSHI

BOKKO-CHAN

Translated by Noriyoshi Saito

The story of a B-girl who didn't have a heart of gold.

The robot was really a work of art. It was a female
robot and, being artificial, she was designed to be the
perfect beauty. Every element that went to make up a
charming girl was taken into consideration. The trouble
was that she looked a little prissy, but who can deny that a
prissy air is an indispensable prerequisite for a beauty?

Nobody else had ever ventured to build such a robot.
Indeed it was silly to build a robot just to do the work of a

man when for an equal amount of expense one could design more efficient machinery or hire suitable workers from among the many whose applications jammed the "Situation Wanted" columns of the classified ads.

However, this robot was made at leisure by the master of a certain bar. A bar-master, in general, will not drink at home at all. For him liquor exists only as his stock-in-trade which should never be consumed for private use. And those haunting drunkards who frequented his bar so willingly helped him to make money with which he was able to spend his off hours in pursuit of a hobby.

It happened that his hobby was the building of a charming robotess.

Since this was his only hobby he spared neither effort nor money in designing her. For instance, she was covered with a skin so smooth that it could hardly be distinguished from that of a real girl. It is no exaggeration to say that she was more enchanting than the genuine beauties around.

Unfortunately, like many great beauties, she was rather empty-headed, since the designing of a complex brain was beyond the capabilities of her inventor. She was able to answer questions of the simplest form and perform simple motions, such as taking a drink.

The bar-master named her "Bokko-chan" and placed her on a chair behind the counter of his bar so that she would not be too close to the customers. He was afraid the robot might show her cloven hoof upon close examination by the patrons of the bar.

So a new girl appeared at the bar and all of the visitors greeted her pleasantly. She behaved satisfactorily until she was asked something other than her name and age. And yet, fortunately enough, nobody noticed she was a robot.

"What's your name, baby?"

"Bokko-chan."

"How old are you?"

"I'm still young."

"Well, how young are you?"

"I'm still young."

"I say, *how* young are you?"

"I'm still young."

Fortunately the patrons of the bar were polite enough not to pursue the question of her age any further.

"Nice dress you wear, huh?"

"Nice dress I wear, don't I?"

"What do you like best?"

"What do I like best?"

"Will you drink a glass of . . . say, gin fizz?"

"I will drink a glass of . . . say, gin fizz."

Bokko-chan never objected to a drink. Nor did she ever become intoxicated.

Charming, young, prissy and smart to chat with. The story of the new girl at the bar spread throughout the neighborhood and the number of visitors to the bar increased. And every visitor enjoyed himself by chatting and drinking with the charming Bokko-chan. Indeed, she seemed to please everyone.

"Whom do you like best among us all?"

"Whom do I like best among you all?"

"Do you like me?"

"I do like you."

"Well, then, shall we go and see some movies?"

"When shall we go?"

Whenever Bokko-chan was asked a question she could not answer she would signal the bar-master who would immediately rush to her side.

"Hey, mister, it's not polite to be flirting with such a baby so much."

The insistent visitor could but grin and retire gracefully under the stern admonition of the bar-master.

The bar-master would sometimes crouch at the foot of
Bokko-chan in which a small plastic spout had been
installed. From this spout he would drain the cocktails that
she had drunk and, being a frugal man, he would serve
them again to the customer. However, the patrons of the
bare were not aware of this and they never ceased to praise
the female robot. They praised her youth and beauty, her
steady character, the fact that she never flattered too much,
and that she never lost her senses from drinking. Thus the
popularity and fame of Bokko-chan grew and grew as did
the number of customers at the bar.

Among the many admirers of Bokko-chan was a young
man whose infatuation with her became so great that he
visited the bar every evening. Night after night he tried to
talk her into going out with him without any success at all.
Her lack of response nearly drove him crazy and he spent
much more than he could afford in an effort to impress her.
His frequent visits to the bar caused him to run up a
considerable bill and when the bar-master called him to
account he attempted to steal from his father in order to
pay his debts.

His father caught him at his attempted theft and a
bitter scene followed during which the father agreed to
advance the young man enough money to pay his debts
provided he would promise never to visit the bar again.

That evening the youth returned to the bar to pay his
bill and, knowing that this was his last visit, he drank much
and treated Bokko-chan.

"I shan't come any more."

"You won't come any more."

"Are you sad?"

"I am sad."

"In reality, you are not, are you?"

"In reality, I am not."

"No other girl is as cold-hearted as you."

"No other girl is as cold-hearted as I."

"Shall I kill you?"

"Will you kill me?"

The youth pulled a pack of drugs from his pocket, poured them into his glass then pushed the glass toward Bokko-chan.

"Will you drink this?"

"I will drink this."

Bokko-chan lifted the glass and drained its contents.

"Go to hell, will you?" the boy said.

"I will go to hell."

The boy quickly settled his bill with the bar-master and ran out into the night.

It was almost closing time and the bar-master was pleased with having collected such a large debt. He drained the liquor from Bokko-chan and set up drinks for all on the bar.

"Drink up, men," said the bar-master, "this is my treat."

The patrons of the bar drank a toast to the bar-master which he acknowledged by draining his own glass.

On that night the lights of the bar were not put out and the radio continued to play music. Nobody departed and yet nobody spoke.

And the time came when the radio said "Good night" as the station sighed off the air.

"Good night," said Bokko-chan waiting with all her prissy air for the next man to call her.

SHINICHI HOSHI

HE–Y, COME ON OU–T!

Translated by Stanleigh Jones

*The discovery of a deep hole
has extraordinary impact on life
in a small town.*

The typhoon had passed and the sky was a gorgeous blue. Even a certain village not far from the city had suffered damage. A little distance from the village and near the mountains, a small shrine had been swept away by a landslide.

"I wonder how long that shrine's been here."

"Well, in any case, it must have been here since an awfully long time ago."

"We've got to rebuild it right away."

While the villagers exchanged views, several more of their number came over.

"It sure was wrecked."

"I think it used to be right here."

"No, looks like it was a little more over there."

Just then one of them raised his voice. "Hey what in the world is this hole?"

Where they had all gathered there was a hole about a meter in diameter. They peered in, but it was so dark nothing could be seen. However, it gave one the feeling that it was so deep it went clear through to the center of the earth.

There was even one person who said, "I wonder if it's a fox's hole."

"Hey—y, come on ou—t!" shouted a young man into the hole. There was no echo from the bottom. Next he picked up a pebble and was about to throw it in.

"You might bring down a curse on us. Lay off," warned an old man, but the younger one energetically threw the pebble in. As before, however, there was no answering response from the bottom. The villagers cut down some trees, tied them with rope and made a fence which they put around the hole. Then they repaired to the village.

"What do you suppose we ought to do?"

"Shouldn't we build the shrine up just as it was over the hole?"

A day passed with no agreement. The news traveled fast, and a car from the newspaper company rushed over. In no time a scientist came out, and with an all-knowing expression on his face he went over to the hole. Next, a bunch of gawking curiosity seekers showed up; one could also pick out here and there men of shifty glances who appeared to be concessionaires. Concerned that someone might fall into the hole, a policeman from the local sub-station kept a careful watch.

One newspaper reporter tied a weight to the end of a long cord and lowered it into the hole. A long way down it went. The cord ran out, however, and he tried to pull it out, but it would not come back up. Two or three people helped out, but when they all pulled too hard, the cord parted at the edge of the hole. Another reporter, a camera in hand, who had been watching all of this, quietly untied a stout rope that had been wound around his waist.

The scientist contacted people at his laboratory and had them bring out a high-powered bull horn, with which he was going to check out the echo from the hole's bottom. He tried switching through various sounds, but there was no echo. The scientist was puzzled, but he could not very well give up with everyone watching him so intently. He put the bull horn right up to the hole, turned it to its highest volume, and let it sound continuously for a long time. It was a noise that would have carried several dozen kilometers above ground. But the hole just calmly swallowed up the sound.

In his own mind the scientist was at a loss, but with a look of apparent composure he cut off the sound and, in a manner suggesting that the whole thing had a perfectly plausible explanation, said simply, "Fill it in."

Safer to get rid of something one didn't understand.

The onlookers, disappointed that this was all that was going to happen, prepared to disperse. Just then one of the concessionaires, having broken through the throng and come forward, made a proposal.

"Let me have that hole. I'll fill it in for you."

"We'd be grateful to you for filling it in," replied the mayor of the village, "but we can't very well give you the hole. We have to build a shrine there."

"If it's a shrine you want, I'll build you a fine one later. Shall I make it with an attached meeting hall?"

Before the mayor could answer, the people of the village all shouted out.

"Really? Well, in that case, we ought to have it closer to the village."

"It's just an old hole. We'll give it to you!"

So it was settled. And the mayor, of course, had no objection.

The concessionaire was true to his promise. It was small, but closer to the village he did build for them a shrine with an attached meeting hall.

About the time the autumn festival was held at the new shrine, the hole-filling company established by the concessionaire hung out its small shingle at a shack near the hole.

The concessionaire had his cohorts mount a loud campaign in the city. "We've got a fabulously deep hole! Scientists say it's at least five thousand meters deep! Perfect for the disposal of such things as waste from nuclear reactors."

Government authorities granted permission. Nuclear power plants fought for contracts. The people of the village were a bit worried about this, but they consented when it was explained that there would be absolutely no above-ground contamination for several thousand years and that they would share in the profits. Into the bargain, very shortly a magnificent road was built from the city to the village.

Trucks rolled in over the road, transporting lead boxes. Above the hole the lids were opened, and the wastes from nuclear reactors tumbled away into the hole.

From the Foreign Ministry and the Defense Agency boxes of unnecessary classified documents were brought for

disposal. Officials who came to supervise the disposal held
discussions on golf. The lesser functionaries, as they threw
in the papers, chatted about pinball.

The hole showed no signs of filling up. It was awfully
deep, thought some; or else it might be very spacious at the
bottom. Little by little the hole-filling company expanded
its business.

Bodies of animals used in contagious disease experiments at the universities were brought out, and to these
were added the unclaimed corpses of vagrants. Better than
dumping all of its garbage in the ocean, went the thinking
in the city, and plans were made for a long pipe to carry it
to the hole.

The hole gave peace of mind to the dwellers of the
city. They concentrated solely on producing one thing after
another. Everyone disliked thinking about the eventual
consequences. People wanted only to work for production
companies and sales corporations; they had no interest in
becoming junk dealers. But, it was thought, these problems too would gradually be resolved by the hole.

Young girls whose betrothals had been arranged discarded old diaries in the hole. There were also those who
were inaugurating new love affairs and threw into the hole
old photographs of themselves taken with former sweet-
hearts. The police felt comforted as they used the hole to
get rid of accumulations of expertly done counterfeit bills.
Criminals breathed easier after throwing material evidence
into the hole.

Whatever one wished to discard, the hole accepted it
all. The hole cleansed the city of its filth; the sea and sky
seemed to have become a bit clearer then before.

Aiming at the heavens, new buildings went on being
constructed one after the other.

One day, atop the high steel frame of a new building

under construction, a workman was taking a break. Above his head he heard a voice shout:

"He—y, come on ou—t!"

But, in the sky to which he lifted his gaze there was nothing at all. A clear blue sky merely spread over all. He thought it must be his imagination. Then, as he resumed his former position, from the direction where the voice had come, a small pebble skimmed by him and fell on past.

The man, however, was gazing in idle reverie at the city's skyline growing ever more beautiful, and he failed to notice.

TAKASHI ISHIKAWA

THE ROAD TO THE SEA

Translated by
Judith Merril and Tetsu Yano

A boy searches for the sea he's never seen.

I must go forth to see the sea!

So the boy resolved. And, the kind of boy he was, no
slings or arrows would stop him once his mind was set.
Without a word to father or to mother he set out from
home.

Which way to the sea? The boy didn't know. But any
which way if he just kept tramping along in one direction,

58

he was bound to come to the sea sooner or later. This was the wisdom of a boy just turned six.

The boy had never seen any sea except inside his picture-books.

. . . *full of blue water everywhere, the open ocean stretches without end. And in it—there's a whale!—and a shark—sea-gills!—a mermaid and an octopus—kelp, coral, and a mole! And over there, and here and here and there again, great floating vans named "ships"—and that one is even a* skull-ship *with* tattooed pirates *riding in it! And the horizon out at sea—water, water, nothing as far as you could see but* water—*what in the world would such a sight look like?* . . .

His mind could not hold on to such a watermuch.

Adrift in dreams of sky-sea-blue, the boy trudged purposefully on.

At the end of the town, he met the old man. This old man was always sitting there by the side of the road, staring at the sky: he was kind of funny in the head.

"Hey, boy!" The old man hailed him, "Where you going?"

"The sea," said the boy, and kept on walking.

"The sea?" The old man opened his toothless mouth and laughed. "That's a good one!" He grabbed the boy by the arm and pulled him to a stop. "Going to the sea? Okay. You'll just have to go to heaven first." He pointed a withered old finger, trembling uncontrollably, at the sky. "The sea is right up there over your head!"

In the clear blue sky there was nothing but the sun, shining bright. The boy didn't say a word. He just pulled loose from the old man and trotted off, pursing his lips a bit and clucking his tongue: *That old man has got too old—his whole head is mixed up now.*

* * *

Pretty soon the boy got to a small hill. Standing on the top of the hill, he looked all around him everywhere, but the presence of the sea was nowhere to be sensed. The boy dropped on his haunches and had something to eat while he watched the gradual shifting of ground-shadows cast by the slow passage of the sun.

Beyond the plain was a range of mountains and the sun was just beginning to slant down in that direction. *The sun sinks in the sea:* that's what he had heard, so—*Let's see what's on the other side!*

The boy straightened his back, set his lips firmly, fastened his eyes on the distant hills, and started walking—

Beyond the mountains were still further mountains. Beyond those mountains stretched a plain. At the far end of the plain, another range of hills confronted him.

The boy kept marching along, all alone. Not one town, not one village, not one person, not one living creature did he meet.

His supplies of food and water were getting sadly low.

He did not understand how the sea should be so far away.

The boy kept going. How many times did he sleep on the ground? It didn't matter. When he was sleeping, when he was walking, he was always seeing his visions of the sea.

He took every shape of the sea. Sometimes he was a fish, sometimes a pirate, another time a harbor, then a sail swelling in the wind—he was always changing from one shape to another; and now—*a storm-toss'd ship, bathed in spray-spume, shot through with lightning bolts, pounded on by thunder-claps, just about to sink at last—*

The boy's legs had stopped walking a while back. Now two moons shed their light on a still small figure stretched out on the red-brown desert sand.

The spacesuit had a two-hundred-hour range before it stopped functioning completely.

The boy was smiling a bit even as his breath stopped. Under the night sky of Mars he lay facing a green star—the sky-floating Earth. The sea was there, but he could never reach it.

Nobody goes back there any more.

MORIO KITA

THE EMPTY FIELD

Translated by
Kinya Tsuruta and Judith Merril

A crowd gathers to witness
a momentous event.

Ground underfootrutcarved with trucktiretrails:
where heavy sculptured treads crisscrossed tired grass

Translators' note: Certain Japanese words have been used here because
they have no precise English equivalents: *Kokoro* means both "heart"
and "mind." Either word alone is insufficient. *Ojisan* is roughly a
combination of mister, mac, sir, uncle, dad, hey you, mate, pops, and
another "sir" for good measure. *Nani-ne* is just what it sounds like in
English.

gives up: piles of gravel, hillocks of sand: at the far end of
the field some children slowly moving silhouettes against
great concrete pipelengths glowing white in encroaching
darkness at the far end of day—mudsmears on cheeks
nearly invisible halfopen mouths seen almost more by ear
than by eye—words more seen then heard—
—murmurous sense as of the underwater conversation
of small fish—
—*can't you stand still?*
—*but! eaten up by gnats!*
—*what gnats? no gnats here!*
—*no?—listen*—
listening: faint many-voiced buzzing—
—*sshhh—listen*—

Brittle silence: dimming light: truckserried surface
like some castoff paperthin dry scaled skin: buzzing?
—*hear anything?*—
—silence, stop-action: vacant field like a deserted
stage after the village play—descent of thick night's curtain
not so much concluding-or-concealing as revealing new
perceptions: whiteness comes to eye—
—at the foot of the hill a cluster of men's shirts flutter
like wash forgotten on the line at night: and it begins
again—
—*what if it really happens?*
—*maybe it's not true?*
—*don't care if it's true or not—if it was just a story we
wouldn't be standing here and whispering*—
—*we could run over there—and yell—and make
faces— and*—

Youngman also stands still as captive audience awash
in airless-whispertide of senseless fish-communication
pouring in through his perhaps-also-halfopen mouth—

—but if it is true?
—then we really run: that way—like locusts!
—either way we run?—we run one way or the other,
sure!—well sure we've been standing still too long
already—
Youngman moves a foot forward again: a step: conscious of movement of legs and of time gone by since he last
walked toward no other purpose than the act itself—
—what would it look like?
—like a snake?—or sea-squirt?—could be no shape at
all—
—nothing like us anyhow!—how do you know?—
dumb! if it was just like us they wouldn't be waiting
there—we wouldn't be waiting here—have to keep still!—
why would we worry about which way to run?
—we could be sleeping like beansprouts in our beds—

Youngman starts past them:
—he too as a boy played in this vacant lot—but then it
was not barren like this: no trace of tiretracks: all green—
tall grasses growing-covering everywhere—
—all body-weight absorbed by thicknesses of grass
underfoot at every step—
—greenshoots moistcool and sensualclinging to foot
touch chest high in grass—grass invaded boy breathing
through grass—

Now—not a single treeleaf on the hill only marching
rows of raw new which-is-whose? company houses—and
the still yawning trench mouth of a bomb-shelter dug
during the war: cave-in-a-cave because the whole hillside
then under bush canopy one green shadowdeep cavern:
magic expanse whose map was traced by busy beetles—

hoe-shaped, armored, others—along the ridged rough bark of an old oak—

 —soundless space where one drop of sap might startle the poised shade-butterfly into flurried flight—tiny figure swallowed by interleafed branchroof arch—

 —and a child-explorer suddenly shrinks into small helplessness drowned in the breathing of the towering trees heart pounding tok!-tok!—

 —*ojisan!*—chipmunk brazenbright boy's voice, dashing the panic child memory—*ojisan: if you go over there they'll just chase you away*—

 —*chase me away?*

 —*the way they look at you*—*!*

 —*like a pregnant stray cat!*

 —*maybe they don't chase grownups*—*maybe they'll let him join*—*join the club*—?

 —*join? club? what club?*—youngman asks.

 —*people waiting up there*—boy's chin jerks toward the hill—*they're waiting a long time for that thing to come down*—

 —*just waiting?*—asks the smallest boy.

 —*well, they can't fly up! so they have to wait for it to come down*—*they're trying to communicate with that machine*—*some new kind of radio thing*—*and there was a voice*—

 —*you heard the voice?*—that very small one asks.

 —*well, they were saying*—

 —*it was different from our voice?*

 —*not like ours, like*—*like a praying mantis*—

 —*ojisan: you going over there?*

No: youngman shakes his head and starts to walk, leaving children behind, skirting sandpiles and pitfalls in the dark, and the dim memories crowding into emptiness:

bare field: open clear spaces of a child's mind: clean empty sponge sucking in from every side, every sign, mixed promise and perception:

—*red clay and concrete pipe become desert and mountain*—for these boys, all children now and in the past, and once himself: in dreams:

—*diving in dew-drenched gravel piles where barren trucktiretrails lead into magic forest heartlands*— youngman walks following such thoughts—

No! wallowing! in *their* fantasies because his own is nothing but a dry and leafless hill, vacant place stripped of wind-flowing grasses—where now in fact lead-legged faltering *kokoro* unstrung he stumbles on ridged real tiretracks chasing trace-memories of diaper-warmth and the creased twilight of the womb:

Understood: the only certainty is entropy.

Ojisan: funny to hear himself called *ojisan*: not the hilarity of the distorted image but instead the sudden secret shock of recognition—nothing to do with years-of-age, just *this-is-I-am-this*: true: skin and guts already drying out and hardened future clear to its farthest horizons—endless detail-realities of everyday laid out through years and years ahead glaringly visible across an empty pace where no trees offer cover.

—*that ojisan*—

—*pretty sour*—

—*aah—grownups get like that*—

—*never want to talk except telling you what you're supposed to do!*

—*why do they get that way?*

—*shrug—no toys?—all tied up tight*—

—*like a fence gate with rusty wire*—

Whispering voices follow and merge with gnat-buzzing fading behind: ahead the darkness thickens more and more: sight and sound dimmed, youngman walks: legs move but *kokoro* stands still stopped in the timeless place of children of all time—these, now, himself, short timeless time ago—burrowing sightless into thickets of dense undergrowth and tumbled pleasure where new worlds within expanding expose yet another burrow-grove entrance to yet another forestworld within—

Just so—just two years back, a student still, his own world turned upon the pivot of himself:
—drinking with a friend, *sake* on tonguetips tingling with vibrant words entangling and coalescing to give life and form to image and idea, whole cosmologies bursting from blind mysteries of youth's sensuality and mounting energy flowering into multitudinous shades and shapes of meaning—
—while all about the absolute brights and darks of the external world crowd in and out.

But I am in-and-out! seed-and-earth, body-and-cell, proton-and-atom—
—proton-self impelled by furious powers to explosion outward slowly slowed, ultimately contained by self-as-integral-atom:
—seedself unripe but fertile rooting in earth of the great-world-self: twisted and warped at present but with sureness of future time: interlinked, earth-seed-self-world in time together can mature.
Just so: so he believed: or had believed?

When?
Awareness faded in these few short days and months—

perhaps from the first time he put on a suit and tied his tie
to go to work—perhaps from that day life began to merge
with the inexorable click of the timeclock, life counted out
in number-counting till even the monotony is hardly felt—
   Busy-ness: time rushing by filled with the smell of
office heaters and screech of traffic brushing against dry
skin: body frozen so still finally even awareness of dryfreeze
evaporates—
   —*you belong to the society?*
   —*nnnhh?*

Two men in the darkness: one young man his own age,
large camera hanging from his shoulder, busy-brisk:
   —*you don't belong to the group meeting here?*
   —*no*—youngman shakes his head.
   Cameraman nods curtly, steps back in darkness with
the other man—a sigh of irritation comes out from one of
them—
   —*come on, let's get out of here!*
   —*give it another thirty minutes—I broke my back
getting here!—let's wait and see if anything—*
   —*you mean nothing, I tell you, nothing's going to
happen!—all we have to do is turn in the picture of these
nuts—*
   —obviously, from some newspaper or magazine: what
for?
   But their business seems less to the point than their
behavior—two people running like mad inside a space the
size of a slow snail's circuit—
   —*no! I have no right to smugness like this—*
   Youngman thinks:
   —the world and all its people follow certain paths
planned or unplanned—

—*and I myself*—can it be, he is the only one untouched by such vibrations?

Youngman wonders—alone inside this dried-and-
packaged existence, does nothing else remain?

If a mushroom cloud went up in front of him, even that
would turn out to be empty—

Youngman expects nothing at all as calmly-surely as
child long back expected-looked to uncover hazy blue skies
inside dark thickets of undergrowth: just so.

Sliding down the slope of the past he has come back to
the same vacant field to find no trace of green growth left:
only trucktracks cruelly dug into dirt.

But not quite so: in some far corners a few clumps of
higher grass still stand and in one clump a dim bulking
shape:

—*you there! watch out*—*a hole there!*

Youngman leans forward watchfully allowing himself
to be steered in around the hole by the dry trickling voice:

—*here you are*—*grass here*—

Youngman takes the indicated seat:

—*nice cool evening*—*enjoying the air here?*

—*nani-ne*—*well, in a way*—*I gave my grandchild
some fish-sausage and got told off for it, so*—

—like the fish-talk of the children, this old man's
words make no more sense then the gnats' buzzing: but
youngman bends a polite ear: dry-and-gentle voice as if the
years have somehow husked it clean on both absurdity and
agony of human busy-ness:

—*I fed the child a bit of fish-sausage, that's all*—
nothing wrong with it—*fish-sausage is tender and
nourishing*—*but my daughter-in-law doesn't like it: doesn't
want me to feed the boy at all*—*she doesn't say anything of
course, not a word out of her mouth: but it's clear enough:*

*I understand—getting old, ears don't matter so—learn to
hear with other senses—*
    Youngman nods absently—

    His own life would soon certainly be consumed with
just such daily non-events—devoured by trivia—like mi-
croscopic worms eating the body from inside till he was left
an impotent old man preoccupied with grandchild and
fish-sausage—
    Youngman laughs politely:—*you live near here?*
    —*live? no*—the husky voice seems to have no age
now—*I come here sometimes—know these parts from very
long ago*—
    —*changed a lot, hasn't it?*
    —*changed?—yes, of course, anything changes*—
    —yet in the vacant lot there is no real change: built up
with factory dormitories or something else in farther future
still it would remain an empty place—

    Lost in perspectives thus youngman continues to
converse—
    —*back in my childhood time grass grew all over
here*—
    —*hill had plenty of trees too*—
    —*talk about that, there were plenty of people on the
hill tonight—?*
    —*yuh—they're still there: waiting for a saucer to come
down.*
    —*what did you say?*
    —*saucer: what they call "sky-flying saucers"*—from
the tone he could be talking about fishcakes still—*that's
what they call them*—

    Youngman peers into darkness at the old man's fuzzed
face: remembers fragments of the children's murmurings—

the journalists' exchange—something about a society to study flying saucers: people who say they meet space-visitors and exchange messages with them—all so ridiculous one does not even really want to laugh—

—*you don't believe in space-men?*

—*well–ll–I don't mind*—youngman, depressed, mumbles potato-mouthed—*suppose it's possible*—

—*yes*—the old man speaks very slowly, softly, seriously—*it is possible.*

No way to answer that—*those people over there—what are they—you know them?*

—*no: no—they're just waiting, that's all—saucer supposed to land over there somewhere—nah, getting old one's ears are bad but*—

—*these people—what makes them think—do they know when—?*

—*of course not—no: it could be any time:*—the statement is quiet and assured.

—*nothing to do with me*—youngman thinks and turns his eyes up to the few stars scattered in the cloud-hazed dark night sky—

—the stars used to have dignity and mystery—now soot and pollution dim their light and no one cares—*people have no time for stargazing anyhow*—

A single point of light shoots suddenly from mid-sky to cross the void: in spite of himself—

—*aa-ahh!*

—*a meteor*—says the old man at his side as if sharing his feelings.

Youngman laughs uneasily eyes still fixed on that corner of the sky: sitting so staring up in the same posture as those others on the hill, youngman's *kokoro* opens:

consciousness—stubborn believers—tense fanatics—seedy
ordinary people—baker, teacher, unemployed perhaps—
staring up to the sky with desperate hope—all this vibrates
through the night into youngman's *kokoro* overflowing:
        —*they must have something to believe in—and I too—*
simply believing is necessary—
        Laugh it away: laughing empties the chest: into the
chasm flows thick night air: long time youngman believes
something not definite but certain things must be:
        —the sky, eternally and infinitely deep: the stars, their
ancient mystery regained: flight of white-silver darts of fire
heating the night sky changing to crimson: hot red rain,
raining—
        —the gleaming transparent shape touches down on
earth noiselessly: strange beings must appear—*like snakes?*
like sea-squirts? without shape?—and everything will
change: cities, towns, worn-out peace, even war: all values
and all meanings—
        —everything must change: and he himself—skin,
bones, spirit must renew themselves cell by cell step by
step—
        —hungry for the first sign of change, youngman gazes
at the sky, waiting, head back, breath caught—
        —*anything the matter?*
        Dry cool old man's voice: dry ice dissolving the brief
fantasy—belief more foolish than child's make-believe—
        Bile burns in his throat: standing up woodenly young-
man stammers:
        —*I'm—get on home*—

        oh you're going?—old man asks quietly—*looks like the*
kids are going too—
        True—over where the concrete pipes gleam white by

night small shadows are detaching themselves one by
one—
    —*everybody's going home, looks like*—the old man is
looking at the hill now: nothing but darkness in that
direction: but the old man nods as if concluding a perfor-
mance and says in dismissal—
    —*well, good night!*

Youngman walks eyes fastened on the sky: thin scattered star-fragments disappear: for already—or perhaps
gathering clouds: dirt underfoot hard-dry and truckdug
tracks every now and then against his sole.
    Alone in the empty place youngman quickens his steps
following the children: still at some distance he feels echoes
of the wash of fish-talk from them—
    —*I knew it—it didn't happen after all—*
    —*it couldn't really—*
    —*they just couldn't make contact, that's all.*
    —*hey! how come we didn't run?*
    —*nothing to run from, you dope!*
    —*running'll wear you down—like dried mushrooms!*
Youngman slows his pace:
    —*it just couldn't happen: nothing can happen.*

Child-shadows disappear—
Youngman's shadow gone—
The cluster at the hill-foot is dissolved.
Behind a clump of weeds, an old man sitting still—
Old man?—not quite that old man now.
Sitting still?—no wind but he is wavering somehow.
Something seems to be changing in the dark.

SAKYO KOMATSU

THE SAVAGE MOUTH

Translated by Judith Merril

A horrific tale by Japan's leading SF writer.

No reason at all.

Why should there be a reason? People want to find
reasons for everything, but the truth of things can never be
explained. All of existence: why *is* it as it is? why just this
way and no other?

That kind of reason, no one would ever be able to
explain. . . .

* * *

Seething with anger, he stood looking out of the window, gritting his teeth. Some days, suddenly, this fury overwhelmed him, suffusing the very centre of his being: a violent irrational urge to destruction which could never be explained to anyone. He jerked the curtain closed: breathing hard he stiffened his shoulders and moved back to the inner room.

The world we live in is worthless, absurd. Staying alive is an absurdly worthless thing. Above all, this worthless character—myself—is quite intolerably absurd.
Why so absurd—?
"Why?" There it was again.
Worthless, absurd, simply *because* absurd and worthless. Everything—prosperity, science, love, sex, livelihood, sophisticated people—nature, earth, the universe—all disgustingly filthy, frustratingly foolish. Therefore—
No. Not "therefore" at all, but *anyhow, I'm actually going to do it.*
I will do it. Rubbing a kink out of his shoulder, he cried out silently: *I really will.*
Of course, this would be just as idiotic as anything else—indeed, among assorted stupidities, maybe the stupidest of all? But at least there was a bit of *bite* to it—a taste of sharpness. Perhaps the result of a touch of madness at the core of the meticulously detailed scheme? Maybe so, but at least—
What I'm going to do now would certainly never have been tried by anyone in his right mind!
Destroy the world? How many tens of thousands of people throughout history must have cherished *that* fantasy! This was nothing so banal. His anger would never be quenched by anything so absurd. *The flames within me are fanned by a truly noble desperation. . . .*

* * *

Entering the inner room, he locked the door, turned
on the light. *Now*—the thought brought a glitter to his
eye—*now it begins*.

The room shone in cool light. In one corner were an
electric range and oven; a gas burner; a slicer; large and
small frying pans; an assortment of kitchen knives; and a
kitchen cabinet stocked with all kinds of sauces and relishes
and vegetables. Next to them was an automated operating
table, fully programmed and equipped to perform any kind
of surgery ever done on the human body—even in the
biggest hospitals, no matter how complex or difficult. And
next to that, a supply of prosthetics: arms, legs, every
available variety of ultra-modern artificial organ.

Everything was ready. It had taken him a full month to
work out the plans in detail, another month to get all the
necessary equipment set up. By his reckoning, it would
take a little more than one additional month until he was all
done.

Right, then—let's get started.

Removing his trousers, he mounted the operating
table, attached monitoring electrodes at several points on
his body, and switched on the videotape.

It begins—

With a dramatic gesture he picked up the syringe lying
on the stand next to the operating table, checked the
pressure gauge, adjusted the setting—a little high, since
this was the first shot—and injected a local anaesthetic into
his right thigh.

In about five minutes, all sensation was gone from the
leg, and he switched on the automatic operating machine.
Buzzing and humming of machinery; tell-tale lights blink-
ing on and off; his body jerked back reflexively as several

extensions emerged from an arm of the shining black machine.

Clamps projecting from the table secured the leg at shank and ankle. A steel claw holding a disinfectant gauze pad came slowly down onto the thigh joint.

The electric scalpel sliced silkily through the skin, cauterising as it went; there was hardly any blood. Cutting the muscle tissue . . . exposing the large artery . . . clamping-off with forceps . . . ligation . . . cutting and treating the contracting muscle surface . . . The buzzing rotary saw was soon whirring toward the exposed femur. It hit the bone; his eyes blinked shut at the shock.

There was almost no vibration. The diamond embedded in the ultra-high-speed saw made only the faintest rubbing noise as it sliced through bone, simultaneously treating the cut surface with a mixture of potent enzymes. In exactly six minutes his right leg had been cleanly severed from the joint.

Wiping his sweat-soaked face gently with gauze, the machine handed him a glass of medicine. He drank it down in a single gulp and drew a deep breath. His pulse was racing; more and more sweat came pouring out. But there was almost no blood lost, and no sensation of anything like pain. The nerve treatments had worked very well. No blood transfusion would be needed. He inhaled a bit of oxygen to ease his dizziness.

His right leg, separated from his body, lay sprawled on the table where it had dropped. A contracted circle of pink muscle tissue surrounded by yellow fat, with red-black marrow at the centre of the white bone, was visible through a tightly wrapped clear plastic dressing. There was almost no bleeding. He stared at the hairy *thing* with its protruding kneecap, and was almost overcome with a fit of hysterical laughter. But there was no time now for laughing: there was more still to be done.

He rested only long enough to recover his energy, then issued instructions for the next part of the job.

The machine extruded a steel arm, picked up an artificial leg and set it in place against the cut surface; the unbandaged treated flesh was already healing. The signal terminal of the artificial synapse centre was connected to a nerve sheath drawn out from the cut surface. Finally, the structural support was firmly attached to the remaining thigh bone with straps and a special bonding agent. *Finished.* He tried bending the new leg cautiously.

So far, so good. He stood up gingerly: It made him dizzy and shaky but he was able to stand and walk slowly. The artificial leg was made out of some kind of lightweight metal that produced a tinny sound when it moved. *All right—good enough*—He'd be using a wheelchair most of the time.

He lifted his own right leg off the top of the table. It was so heavy he was almost staggering. Inside himself, he was once again seized with a paroxysm of savage laughter. *All my life I've been dragging all this weight around.* How many kilos had he liberated himself from by cutting off this support?

"All right," he muttered to himself, still giggling. "Enough. Now to drain the blood. . . ."

Carrying the heavy joint over to the workbench he stripped off the plastic wrap and hung the leg from the ceiling by the ankle, squeezing it through his hands to start the blood dripping from the cut end.

Later, washing it in the sink, with the hairs plastered down by the water, it looked more like the leg of a giant frog than any other kind of animal. He stared at the sole of the foot poking grotesquely over the edge of the stainless steel sink.

My leg. Protruding kneecap, hard-to-fit high instep, toes infested with athlete's foot—*That's my leg!* And he was finally completely carried away, bent double in an uncontrollable spasm of poisonous laughter. *At last there will be an end to that damned persistent athlete's foot . . .*

Time to get ready for the cooking.

He used the big slicer to cut the leg in two at the knee, then began stripping off the skin with a sharp butcher's knife. The thigh-bone was thick with delicious-looking meat. *Of course: it's the ham.* The tendons were stiff; he was covered with sweat as he worked the hand-slicer, quickly piling up large chunks of meat surrounded by muscle membrane. He put chunks of shinmeat to simmer in a big pot filled with boiling hot water, bay leaf, cloves, celery, onions, fennel, saffron, peppercorns and other spices and savoury vegetables. The foot he threw out, keeping only the meat scraped out of the arch. The ham he sliced up for steak, rubbing in salt and pepper and plenty of tenderiser.

Will I have the courage to eat it? he asked himself suddenly. Tough lumps always stuck in that spot in his throat. Would he really be able to stomach it?

He clenched his teeth, oozing oily sweat. *I will eat.* It was no different from the way human beings had always cooked and eaten other intelligent mammals: cows and sheep, those gentle, innocent, sad-eyed grass eaters. Primitive man even ate his own kind; some groups had practised cannibalism right up to modern times. Killing an animal *in order to eat*—perhaps there was some justification for that. Other carnivores had to kill to live too. But human beings . . .

Since the day they came into existence, through all of human history, how many billions of their fellows had people killed *without even eating them?* Compared to that, this was positively innocent! *I'm not going to kill anyone else. I'm not going to slaughter miserable animals. This way, what I myself eat is my own meat.* What other food could be so guiltless?

The oil in the frying pan was beginning to crackle. With shaking hands he grasped a great piece of meat, hesitated, hurled it in. Crackling fat began to flood the air with savoury smells. Still trembling, he was gripping the arms of the wheelchair so hard he almost snapped them.

All right. I am a pig. Or rather, human beings are much worse than pigs: filthier, nastier. *Inside myself there is a part that is less-than-pig, and a "noble" part endlessly angry and ashamed at being less-than-pig.* That "noble" part was going to eat the "less-than-pig" part. What was there to fear in that?

The crisply browned slice of meat sizzled on the plate. He smeared mustard over it, applied lemon and butter, poured gravy on top of that. When he made to use the knife, his hand was dancing so that it set the plate to clattering. Streaming with sweat, he gripped the knife with all his strength, sliced, jabbed the fork, and carried *It* fearfully into his mouth.

On the third day, he amputated the left leg. This one, just as it was, shinbone and all, he skewered and smeared liberally with butter, then roasted it on the rotisserie in the big oven. He was fearless by now. He had discovered himself to be surprisingly delicious: with that discovery, a mixture of anger and madness rooted itself firmly in his heart.

After the first week, things got more difficult. He had to amputate the lower half of his body.

On the toilet installed in the wheelchair, he experienced the delights of defecation for the last time in this world. As he ejected, he guffawed.

Look at this mess! What I am now excreting is my own self, stored up in my own bowels and turned to shit! Perhaps this was the ultimate act of self-contempt—or might it be the utmost in self-glorification?

The gluteus maximus was the most delicious of all.

With everything from the hips down gone, the last usefulness of the artificial legs was also gone, but he left them in place for the time being. Now that it was time for the internal organs, he consulted the machine's electronic brain: "When I have eaten the intestines, will I still have an appetite?"

"It will be quite all right," was the reply.

He discarded the large intestines, put the small intestines into a stew with vegetables, and used the duodenum to make sausages. He replaced the liver and kidneys with artificial organs, then ate the originals in a sauté. The stomach he set aside until later, preserved in a plastic container filled with nutritive fluids.

At the end of the third week, he exchanged his heart and lungs for artificial organs, and at last ate his own pulsing heart, fried in thin slices: a deed beyond even the imaginations of the priests of the Aztec sacrificial rituals.

By the time he made a meal of his own stomach— soaked in soy sauce, with garlic and red pepper—he had come to understand clearly that *people are quite capable of eating with no need for food*.

In the wide range of varied and exotic products people

used for food, how many had been discovered out of curiosity, and not from hunger at all? Even when their curiosity is satisfied, humans will eat the most unimaginable things, *as long as there was anger.* In a fit of fury, eating the flesh of one's own kind can be like crushing a glass with one's teeth . . .

The well-springs of appetite lie in the savage impulse for aggression: killing-and-eating, crushing-and-crunching, swallowing-and-absorbing— *that is the savage mouth.*

By now, the end of his throat was connected only to a disposal tube. Nourishment for the remaining body tissues was poured directly into the blood from a container of nutritive fluids; endocrine functions were maintained with the help of artificial organs.

By the end of the month, both arms were completely eaten; the only part that remained was from the neck up. And by the fortieth day, almost all the muscles of the face had been eaten as well: the lips alone were left to chew with the assistance of attached springs. Only one eyeball remained; the other had been sucked and chewed.

What sat there now, mounted on a labyrinthian mechanism of pipes and tubes, was the living skull alone: in that skull, only mouth and brain survived.

No . . .

Even now, an arm of the machine was peeling off the scalp, taking a saw to the top of the skull and removing it cleanly.

Sprinkling salt and pepper and lemon on the trembling exposed cerebrum, in the act of scooping up a great spoonful—*My brain,* thought the cerebrum-that-was-he. *How can I taste such a thing? Can a man live to savour the taste of his own brain-jelly?*

The spoon punctured the ashy-hued brain. No pain—

there is no sensation in the cerebral cortex. But by the time the arm of the machine scooped up that pale mushy paste and carried it to the skull's mouth, and the mouth lapped it up to swallow, "taste" was no longer recognizable.

"Homicide," the Inspector told the reporters crowded into the entrance-way as he came out of the room. "And what's more, an almost unprecedentedly brutal and degenerate crime. The criminal is probably a medically knowledgeable psychopath. Looks like an attempt at some sort of insane experiment—the body was taken apart limb from limb, and hooked up to all kinds of artificial organs. . . ."

The Inspector disposed of the press and went back into the room, wiping his face from exhaustion.

The detective came over from the incinerator and eyed him questioningly. "The tapes are burned," he said, "but—why are you calling it murder?"

"For the sake of maintaining peace and order." The Inspector took a deep breath. "Declare it murder—conduct an official investigation—and leave it shrouded in mystery. This case—releasing the facts as they are in this case—it goes against all reason! You can't make ordinary decent citizens look into the pits of madness and self-destruction hidden away at the bottom of some people's minds. If we did such a thing—if we carelessly exposed people to a glimpse of the savage beast lurking inside—well, you can be sure someone else would try to follow this guy's example. These kind of people—*there's no way to know what they're capable of.* . . .

"If the general public was suddenly made aware of something like this, people would begin to lose confidence in their own behaviour—they'd start probing and peering at the blackness inside their own souls. They'd get entirely out of their depths—completely out of control!

"You see, what is at the root of human existence is *madness*—the blind aggressive compulsion that lies in wait at the heart of all animals. If people become conscious of this—if really large numbers of people start expressing that madness under slogans like *existential liberation* and *do your own thing*—we're done for! It's the end of human civilization. No matter what kind of law or force or order we try to work with, it'll get completely out of control!

"People tearing themselves apart, killing each other, wrecking, destroying—the symptoms are already beginning to show up—this one commits suicide by swallowing fused dynamite—that one pours gasoline and sets himself on fire— another starts screwing in the middle of the city in broad daylight. When there is nothing more reasonable left to attack, the caged animal starts to destroy his own sanity— "

"Yaa-a-a!"

The young detective screamed and jumped back from the rotting skull. He had been about to remove the foul-smelling spoon still held between the lips when the skull sank its teeth into his finger, nipping off a pinch of meat from the tip.

"Be careful," said the Inspector wearily. "The foundation of all animal life is a great starving swallowing savage mouth. . . ."

The skull, with its naked brain, its one remaining eye beginning to come loose, and strong springs replacing its vanished muscles, was now slowly crumpling and chewing the scrap of meat between its swollen tongue and sturdy teeth.

SAKYO KOMATSU

TAKE YOUR CHOICE

Translated by
Shiro Tamura and Grania Davis

The ultimate escape:
a one-way ticket to the future.

At first he thought he'd been following the streets as he'd been directed, but he seemed to have missed the landmark somewhere along the way, as he wandered here and there among the intricate alleyways and back streets. Now he was unable to find his way.

Since he could think of no other way out, he decided to leave the squalid tangle of back streets and go back to the main street, where he could start again from the very beginning. But no sooner had he started walking than the landmark appeared.

But the appearance of the shop before him was quite different from what he'd been told. The man who described the shop said that it was for underwater swimming equipment. This shop was apparently a secondhand shop packed with old fashioned robots and two-dimensional TV sets now considered almost antique.

However, he decided to speak to the elderly man in the shop who seemed to be the proprietor.

"Can I take a choice?"

The elderly man with too shiny hair, which was doubtless a wig, turned his lusterless eyes from the three-dimensional TV set that he'd been watching. One of his eyes was an ash-colored electron-glass eye which was oddly distorted sideways.

"Have some kind of introduction from someone?" asked the elderly proprietor unamiably.

He produced from his pocket a piece of paper with a strange sign on it, which he got from his acquaintance as a token of introduction, and a five credit bill.

The elderly proprietor looked at the sign on the paper, then he put it under a machine that resembled a check examiner—then he put the five credit bill into his pocket and stood up to open the door at the end of the room.

"Please . . ." The elderly proprietor showed him the way, thrusting out his chin.

"Are you remodeling the shop?" he asked. "I heard that it was shop for underwater swimming equipment."

"Oh *that*! There's another entrance facing the other side of the block," explained the elderly proprietor. "It's just opposite the next block of buildings—so you came back here by mistake. But it's all the same once you're inside the shop."

Behind the door were steep stairs going downward. Pointing his forefinger toward the door at the foot of the stairs, the elderly proprietor said, "It's inside that door. It's pretty dark down there, but you keep on walking straight as there will be only one corridor—mind your step."

It was quite understandable that he gave such a warning, for if you looked carefully, the stairs were made of prefabricated feather-weight framing structures used for scaffolding at building sites. It appeared so fragile that if your fingernail should accidentally catch any part sticking out of the structure, it would likely fall into pieces, he thought.

The walls weren't illuminated, but there was an outdated fluorescent lamp hanging from the ceiling. At his every step and movement, the stairs trembled and made loud creaking noises. The stairs were on wheels and the entrance had recently been installed, so he concluded that the whole structure could be removed at a moment's notice if necessary.

As soon as he opened the odd looking hatch-like iron door at the bottom of the stairs, he smelled unpleasantly damp air surrounding him. He guessed that there must be a hidden ion air-cleaning device working somewhere, but even so the place didn't deceive him for he sensed a sewerish atmosphere, even though it was furnished with a red carpet and the walls in a subtle color were attractive enough. Judging from the feel of the floor, he was sure this corridor was a prefabricated structure.

It smells rotten, he thought—but if it is really . . . Again there was another door at the end of the corridor. When he knocked on the door, he thought he heard the clicking sound of a camera-eye blink, then the door opened solemnly—this door seemed unnaturally dignified.

Inside the door was an oblong waiting room, as if it

were still a continuation of the corridor. It looked rather
like the inside of a lounge-type, old fashioned railroad car.
The floor was furnished with a dark green carpet which
looked luxurious at first sight, but the furniture was of very
poor taste, and a flashy three-dimensional TV set was
mounted on the wall. It still looked like a special private
coach compartment, despite all that. If he had visited a red
light district a long time ago, it would have reminded him
of a brothel waiting parlor. He sniffed and frowned a bit as
he eyed the furniture—he hesitated for a moment deciding
whether to sit on a grimy looking chair and didn't dare to do
it. While he was still standing beside the chair, the door of
the next room was opened by a little man with dull eyes
asking him to come in. "This way, please."

Wondering how many doors he must go through, he
followed the man into the next room. At first sight, he
thought he'd come to the dead end of the passage he'd been
through, but then he noticed that there again were three
doors on the wall beyond a big desk in front of him.
Observing carefully, he noticed that the upper part of the
doors appeared to be a screen of some kind.

"Please sit down." The little man with the absent-
minded expression spoke to him with the same vague voice
as before.

As he sat on the chair facing the desk, he expected to
see an office manager appear from one of these doors, but
none of them opened. Instead the little man with the
vacant look who'd admitted him walked around the desk
and comfortably seated himself on the chair.

"Has anyone given you an introduction. . . ?" asked
the small man with the vacant face—this was partly because
his grey-white eyes were unmistakably crossed.

When he mentioned the token name of the stranger

he'd met at a bar where he learned about this place, the little man languidly nodded.

"I see—it seems all right. Yes, he's one of my trusted friends," said the little man. "By the way . . . are you prepared to pay the full fee here?"

"Yes, I've brought the money with me," he said. "Two million five hundred thousand credits, isn't it?"

"By check or in cash?"

"Credits in cash—in small units."

"Good." The little man nodded but stopped him from taking his wallet from his pocket. "No, that's not necessary for the moment. You can pay later. It's such a large sum of money, you should pay the fee when you actually do it."

He thought this was merely a gesture on the part of this shabby-looking man—but of course there's no point hurrying to pay, so he removed his hand from his pocket.

"Well . . ." The little man with his chin in his palms gave him a sharp look. "How much do you know about this thing?"

"I heard that one can choose his future or something like that."

"Is that all?"

"Y-yes . . ."

The little man stood up and rubbed his head with one hand, chewing a fingernail at the same time. "That would be a bit difficult," he said. "I don't know exactly what you have in mind—but it won't be as fantastic as you imagine. It will only have a subtle effect on your immediate future life. It really isn't such an exiting discovery or anything, since it came about rather by pure chance."

"Whatever it is, explain it to me will you. . . ?" he said eagerly. In fact his curiosity was aroused by the little man's reluctant attitude—though that also might be a trick.

"Then I'll tell you the truth. I—and my partner, too—aren't people of this present world."

"Then you are. . . ?" He had to swallow hard before he could say it. "By any chance you are . . . ?"

"Yes, we are. We're from the future, so to speak. We've time traveled as sort of escapees or violators of the time traveler control laws in our world."

He wondered if what he'd just heard was at all true, as he gazed intently at the little man. In his appearance there was nothing remarkably different from us, except his vagueness and a slipshod manner in his behavior.

"Then?" he urged the man.

"So then by producing in this world a more powerful time travel mechanism with prolonged mobility, we could fly into a time and place which would be beyond the control of our Time Authorities. We would simply fade somewhere into the intricate network of time."

"Wait a moment!" he interrupted. "Why are you in trouble with. . . ?"

"You couldn't understand the strictness of the time travel regulations, no matter how hard I try to explain it." The little man shook his head sadly. "In order to get a permit, we must go through all sorts of red-tape procedures, and a most demanding inspection is required. Above all, we must always be with an official guide of the Time Travel Control Department. An individual time-traveling alone is an act of first class crime in our society."

"Well, that's adequate," he nodded. "I can't understand the ways of your society. Those who lived in a car-less era would never be able to comprehend the offense of excessive speeding on the highways. But choosing one's future—by using your time mechanism?"

"Well, no, not exactly. Strictly speaking, it's done through the use of certain functions of the mechanism—

only the time-space channel selector and time-scope are needed."

"I don't think I follow you."

"If you aren't aware of the fundamentals of time travel, it's very difficult to explain it to you. Anyway, we can't use the drive energy of the mechanism too readily. In short, we can't afford to put you in the machine and send you into the future or past worlds. If we did that, the wave impact of the mechanism in motion would attract the attention of the Time Patrol."

"I see. Then. . . ?"

"Then we can use the time-space channel. That is, we merely have to make a whole of part of a multi-dimensional area—so it's really nothing difficult."

"Do you think you could explain that more simply?" he said, feeling slightly irritated. "Why on earth will that lead to a choice in my future?"

"It's something to do with why one can time-travel," said the little man with a sympathetic smile. "Any explanation would be incomprehensible for you, I'm afraid, so I'll make it more symbolic. Did you know that our world and our history aren't the only possibilities? There are infinite possibilities into the past or into the future existing side by side."

"No. . . I didn't," he answered vaguely. "But I think I've heard something like that before, and it isn't impossible to conceive of an idea like that—to a certain extent."

"You see, it's similar to the theory in non-Euclidian geometry that you can draw unlimited numbers of lines parallel to a line passing a point— which aren't on the line. Because of that, in the early age of time travel, there were many incidents in which travelers didn't return to the time-space point of departure after their trip to the future or the past. For instance, suppose you are starting from the point P to a certain point A in the future. This future isn't the only possibility of A extended from point P, there are also A_2, A_3, A_4 . . . an infinite number of possibilities into the future. Anyway, you go to a point A in one future among the others, but when you try to return to the starting point by descending the time ladder to the past, you often find yourself unable to do so. Because the course from point A to the past is also divided into unlimited numbers of P_2, P_3 . . . P_n."

"I see." He gave a disgusted look of faked comprehension. "So?"

"To avoid such a labyrinth effect, the time-space channel selector was invented, which uses a kind of resonance phenomenon. By making use of the time-space resonance between point A and point P and driving the time mechanism along the resonance channel, you can travel from P to A, and then return from A to P without going astray. But with this method you can't go into the future or past worlds which are variably spread as unlimited numbers of branches—you have access only to several channels at the resonance juncture, depending on the efficiency of the oscillator. The more powerful an oscillator is, the more channels you will have. *Our* time mechanism has only three channels."

At last he began to understand a little. "Therefore," he said, "I can choose my future. Am I right?"

"Well, yes, in a manner of speaking," nodded the little man. "This channel selector will give you a direction from this very room in this world at this moment towards three possible directions into the future. But this only gives you a certain direction, so your choice of a future world won't immediately materialize. You can take your choice among the future worlds we offer, and we send you into the channel of your choice. Then from that point on, among all the possible future worlds to which we have access, you, your surroundings, and the history of the entire world will move in a certain direction."

"In other words . . ." The words stuck in his throat. "There are three different passages into the future from this room, aren't there?"

"Exactly." The little man pointed a finger behind him. "An oscillator is installed behind those three doors, and once you go through one of the channel doors there will be a time-space world with a distinct direction toward its future."

"What are these three future worlds? Will I learn about them in advance?" He leaned forward as he felt his voice begin to tremble with excitement.

"One moment, please . . ." The little man reached his hand under the desk. "I'll show you a bit of the future world by operating the time scope along the channels."

The room suddenly became dark. The upper panels of the three doors began to shine with pale light. "From the right-hand corner these are numbers one, two, and three history courses," said the little man. "Starting number one, then . . ." The door panel on the right-hand side shone brighter than before. "The upper part of the panel is the time scope . . ."

There was something moving in the light, then it slowly took shape—it resembled a three-dimensional color TV set, he thought.

The scene appearing on the screen was that of a future city being built vigorously, at incredible speed. Covered by a bubble-dome, there were buildings of various shapes; a circular cone, a honeycomb pattern, a cylinder and ball— which themselves were cities, joined by pipeways spreading among them like the meshes of a spider's web.

Without any visible device, people themselves were

flying in the air—perhaps by using a gravity control device—and a huge rocket, also a city, was heading for a planet or star. Factories, buildings and artificial land were spreading over the surface of the earth, now orbited by a large number of man-made satellite cities.

"Seen enough?" asked the little man.

"All right," he murmured. "Second course, please . . ."

The second door panel began to glitter. It was a kind of Restoration scene. The city was far more simple in its designs than in the first scene, and buildings weren't soaring into the sky, but were distributed harmoniously among the scenic beauties of nature. Roads bordered with beautiful flowers and trees were spaciously etched on the land. Gracefully designed cars were moving slowly on the wide roads, while producing no exhaust fumes, noise or dust.

People's clothes were also simple, but the men were handsome as Adonis, and all the women had a nymph-like appearance. The sun, shimmering and golden, seemed to be artificial, and the climate seemed to be under human control. But the machines and all devices seemed harmoniously designed, though most of them were hidden behind the classical facade of the city. Its appearance showed the most beautiful moment of the history it had reached.

Athletic meetings were being held in stadiums and pools, while music played continuously at outdoor concert halls. Recitations of poetry were taking place in public salons where any passerby could drop in freely. Among the white clouds in the sky there was a swan-shaped aircraft with a gravity control device, floating like a waterbird on a lake . . .

"Classical esthetic harmony . . ." he murmured. "They must have made some daring artificial changes."

"Next—may I?" the little man asked.

"Please . . ." he answered.

The screen of the third door panel didn't brighten for a while—but there was a sense of something busily moving behind the dim light. Soon there appeared a city and its people walking in confusion this way and that. It seemed to him that the appearance of this city wasn't much different from the present world. Dust, smog, bustling streets, dingy-looking tall buildings, decaying apartment buildings that had become slums . . .

But somewhere above the city there was a sense of uneasiness. People's faces were tense with inexplicable anticipation mixed with anxiety, impatience and resignation. Suddenly at the corner of the street someone shouted as he looked up at the sky. The tensed faces of the fearful people turned at once in the same direction.

Immediately after that, a blinding flash beamed on the screen and he had to turn his face from it. The light was strong that it left some red and green hazy images in his eyes for a while, and he could see nothing else.

"Is that all?" he asked.

"No, not yet; there's a bit more to it," the little man's voice was heard from the darkness near him. "Here comes the scene."

At first he couldn't make out what it was. Something like a big black stain. It took sometime for him to realize that it was actually a gigantic hole that covered the entire city. Around the burnt-out hole there were ruins—looking like mere masses of melted glass which spread for several miles, and even the mountains in the far distance were turned into masses of molten rock. Within several hundred miles of the crater no grass or trees or perhaps even bacteria survived, not to mention birds and animals. Every sign of life in the area was gone. High in the sky there hung the reddish-brown colored clouds of radioactive dust being blown by the wind.

Tidal waves struck everywhere and typhoons were born by the thousands. There was no sign of surviving human beings, as if they'd never existed at all. It seemed that they'd turned into a heap of carbon or light ashes, and most of them must now be floating in the air as a mass of lethal radioactivity.

The light was turned on and the image on the screen faded.

"Well," said the little man in his usual indifferent, monotonous voice. "These are the three possible futures that our time-space channel selector can contact. Whichever you fancy—take your choice, please."

"I have a question," he said, his voice a little husky. "What's the distance in time to the era just seen on the screen of what you call a time scope?"

"These three are almost the same distance from the present time. They aren't really very distant futures. The distance in time covered by this time scope isn't always the same, but it's more or less between several years ahead to a little more than a decade into the future—perhaps twenty years ahead of us at maximum."

"One more thing," he said. "Can I come back here at all?"

"I'm afraid you can't do that. To return to this world you'd need a time mechanism." The little man yawned slightly as he spoke. "Well now, take your choice, please. . . ."

He thought for a moment or two then said, "Number two seems like a good choice."

"Then we'd like to charge you the fixed fee," said the little man. "You might think it's a very large sum, but you may consider it as some sort of donation to the liberalists from the future world—to help their escape."

He took out his bulging wallet and paid the little man the amount of money charged.

"I'm going to open the door of channel two now. . . ." The little man put the money into a drawer and stood up. "And there are things we want you to be aware of after you've selected your future."

He felt his forehead sweating unreasonably hard. Wiping it with the back of his hand, he looked again at the three doors in turn, comparing them carefully.

"As I told you many times, this will only give you a certain direction towards your future, but you're not going to be sent immediately into the future world that you've just seen on the screen. You see, we must make sure that you don't misunderstand that point. For this reason, the world beyond this door won't be any different from this present world you're now in. Your everyday life, the city, family and friends, all of those will be exactly the same as in this world. But of course there will be some changes taking place in the future, and as time passes it will become different from all the other worlds, and will definitely more towards the future you've just seen. And . . ."

"Excuse me . . ." he said hesitatingly, in a quiet voice.

"And you must promise us one thing. We'd like you to keep your mouth shut in the world of the other side, about the fact that you've come from this side and met us here. It wouldn't do you any harm, nor would it give you any advantage if you told the whole story, but we're bound to get in trouble if any of the Time Patrolmen secretly mingle among the people of that era and learn about this operation here. Please promise me not to say a word about this, will you? Now . . ."

"Just a moment . . ." he said. "Can I still change my choice?"

"Well, I suppose you could, but . . ."

"Let me see the three future worlds once more, will you?"

The little man switched on the machine again. Watching the scenes simultaneously appear on the three door panels, he swallowed hard.

"All right," he said in a painful voice. "I've made up my mind. It'll be number three."

"Did you say *number three?*" the little man replied with some amazement. "That's an odd choice to make. As you see, this is just . . ."

"I know," he answered, wiping the cold sweat off his face. "The other two futures are so predictable that they will be realized sooner or later even if I don't try to create them by paying a large sum of money."

"The third one might well be the same, don't you think?"

"No . . ." Painfully clearing his throat he continued, "Rather than living in an uncertain world where a holocaust is always present as a possibility, I think I can be at ease in a world where the holocaust is sure to take place. What's more, I feel that this future isn't so easily obtainable by other means. A world that will *certainly see its holocaust while I'm alive*— such a world . . ."

"As you like . . ." The little man shrugged. "There are many customers who've said the same thing. Then please come to the front of the number three door."

Feeling his mouth drying, he advanced towards the third door.

The thought that he was taking such an irrevocable step made his whole body tense. *Get back!* an inner voice shouted. *What a foolish choice you're making! It's not too late yet. Get back!*

His entire body—every living cell, all resisted with their total strength against the choice that would bring him certain death. Even so, he was still standing in front of the third door as he nervously rubbed his hands. He was now drenched with sweat.

"Now please . . ." said the little man in a disinterested voice. "Beyond this door is a passage. You may feel some discomfort when you enter the time-space channel, but it won't be unbearable, I assure you. Go straight. At the end of the passage there will be another door, and on the other side is a room exactly the same as this one. Its appearance is the same—but it won't be on this side any longer. You won't have any trouble over there. You'll be able to live the same life that you've been leading in this world. That is . . . for the time being. Now, good luck."

With a faint creaking noise, the door opened. Shivering as if suffering from a fever, he walked towards the darkness that now opened in front of him—as though he were pulled by some unseen string.

Get back! Such words still echoed somewhere inside his body, but he kept on walking. He didn't notice when he'd passed the entrance, but suddenly he heard the door slam shut behind him, and he was now in total darkness. Frantically he groped in the darkness and looked back at the door he'd just entered.

But he was surrounded by utter blackness, and he couldn't even tell how wide the place was. He began to move very slowly, step by step. The passage was a gentle slope going downward. As he walked, the floor of the passage abruptly became soft like jelly. It was so sudden that he lost his balance and crashed into a wall. He felt peculiar vibrations all around him, and he couldn't help feeling sick with a painful headache and giddiness.

He felt as if the darkness itself began to revolve around

him, but he kept on walking with gritted teeth, though he often lost his balance and crashed here and there as he tried to advance.

When he finally recovered, he was leaning against something cold. He touched it with his hand; it seemed to be an iron door. He had finally reached the end of the passage.

He knocked on the door as many times as he was told, and the door opened without a sound. For a while he couldn't see anything because of the blinding brightness that filled the room, so he stood there with unsteady feet. Beyond the door was just as the little man had told him; a room which appeared exactly the same as the last one.

At first he was under the false impression that he had returned to the original room. But soon he noticed that the room was one that belonged to the world of the other side because there was only one door in this room, though there had been three in the previous room from which he'd just exited.

"Welcome to this world . . ." said a little man—actually not the same little man, but a little man belonging to this world—but with the same dull voice as before. "This is the way out, please."

"Before I leave, I'd like to ask you one thing," he finally said with some difficulty. "I've just come from the world of the other side. If that is the case, what will happen to the relation between the other 'I', who was originally in this world, and myself? Won't we clash in some way?"

"Oh, that's OK, don't worry . . ." the little man told him in a tired manner. "It would be a long story if I had to explain it, but anyway we've sent another 'you' belonging to this world into the world you were living in before, through a certain method—so there's no problem."

"But how did you. . . ?"

"This is the way out, please," said the little man. "Goodbye."

He sensed there was no more chance for him to get further explanations, so he left the room without argument. The same corridor, the same stairs and second-hand shop— he walked through all these and came out to the same dingy back streets where he'd walked before.

The place looked exactly the same as the one he'd just been through. Every detail of the scene was the same, even the scribbling on a fence and the thickness of the clouds in the sky.

But—he knew. This world was destined to be cut off from its future at some point by an inevitable holocaust. That was a fact known only to him—and to those others who had chosen door number three from those three doors. This secret was the sort of thing that most of the populace would never have dreamed of.

I am the only one, he said to himself as he looked up at the polluted sky of the city. *No one except me definitely knows the fate of this world. Several years, or perhaps a decade from now—I will see that blinding flash of light above this city, and everything will come to an end. What absolute certainty!*

Unlike those other two worlds beyond the doors, this world has no future after that. There will be no tedious, prolonged years that will be recorded as an infinite repetition of daily life. When seen in that light, every aspect of the city—scattered litter, a snotty urchin, wandering stray dogs and even flashing sign-boards, everything was framed in pathetic outline. It seemed to him as though they were delineated by the vivid and sharp lines of death and destruction. And for the first time in ten years he felt clarity, liveliness and tragic satisfaction filling his heart.

With a steady gait he began to walk towards an area of

the city that knew nothing—but was moving poignantly towards the inevitable holocaust of the future . . . his future.

"We're making a fortune, my friend," said the little man as he took out a cash credit ledger from the desk. "It's nearly a billion now. Are we going to continue doing this?"

"Of course," said the other man, the friend. "Our boss is also happy with the results. Anyway, there's no other scam as profitable as this, right? Time machine and time channel . . . well, aren't we clever to make up such a story! We use a pipe from a sewer and if we get into trouble by any chance, we'll simply disappear. But I'm sure it's going to be OK for quite a while."

"That's right," said the little man with his vague voice. "Going to be more customers day after day, and if we stick to this method no one will suspect us. Since each one believes that he's in another world, no one opens his mouth. Above all, they're afraid of being looked at as complete nuts if they try to tell a story like that."

"Time-space channel . . ." said his pal with a chuckle. "Using only ordinary doors of no special value and shop-worn SF films— don't you think that's pretty good? Ask them to step in the door with an air of importance. Make them faint once in the next small room with an anesthetic gas and a vibrating device, and when they come out through the very same door, we make sure they think they're in another world. You know, people are so funny. When they enter the next room, we show them three doors and when they come out we hide the two other doors with curtains, and that's all they need to make them believe they've come into a different room. Nobody suspects or tries to check the room."

"But, my friend," the little man said in a subdued voice, "there's one thing bothering me a bit . . ."

"Our boss says he's going to set up more branches throughout the world," the friend said in a lordly manner. "As long as we've got customers, we're going to make money. There are already 400 'shops' in the world, and there'll be more to come. So what's bothering you?"

"The other day at headquarters I had a look at the statistical data," said the little man, frowning. "One after another, most of the customers choose door number three. Why is that? It's the same here—nearly every one of them chooses number three after a moment of hesitation."

"That shows, contrary to one's expectations, that people have a strong desire for destruction," the friend chuckled. "Though they may speak of peace and humanism when they open their mouths, in their minds—consciously or otherwise—they all want to witness the end of the world— the final dramatic holocaust, rather than a tedious thriving, if they can vanish with the others without suffering. People are, in one way or another, very lewd. Can't help having a wish to peep. To satisfy this secret lustful desire for peeping, they don't care if the world is blown up. So that's what they are—but it's going to be OK. It'll be a long time before they finally realize that they've been deceived. Probably not for a decade, right?"

"But my friend," said the little man with a hollow voice, "already, just at our store alone, more than several thousand people have all gone through door number three. In the coming years, if those people increase at this rate, what's going to happen to the world? If the people who believe that this world will definitely be finished in little more than a decade are going to increase in large numbers all over the world. . . ? You know, among our customers there were many officials, officers, politicians. . . ."

TENSEI KONO

TRICERATOPS

Translated by David Lewis

*A funny thing happened on the way home
—a dinosaur crossed our path.*

The father and son were returning from cycling. They
had set out together on a Sunday of deepening autumn,
heading for the cycling course along the river. On the way
back they had been forced to burrow through the exhaust
and dust of the national highway before finally reaching the
residential area a mile from home. Their house lay beyond
this slightly aging neighborhood, on the other side of the
small hill, in the new subdivision. It was only a little past

104

seven, but the autumn sun was sinking quickly and darkness had begun to gather about them. The father and son stopped their bikes beneath the yellow light of the streetlamps and breathed the cool air in deeply.

"Are you okay, Dad?"

"My knees are ready to fall apart. Let me rest a minute."

"I don't feel a thing."

"I guess you wouldn't," said the father. He smiled wryly as he lit a cigarette.

"Somebody's making curry!" his son cried suddenly. "I'm starving to death. Can't we go now? It's just a little bit farther."

"I guess so."

The father crushed out the cigarette with the tip of his shoe and put his hands back on the black handlebars. It was at the instant the father and son had put one foot to the pedals, at the instant they were looking down the road ahead of them, were beginning to gather momentum, a huge shadow darted across the intersection no more than five or six meters away, shaking the very earth as it passed.

It had the feeling of mass, of power, of a bulldozer, of a ten-ton truck.

Though its passage took but an instant, it indelibly burned on their eyes an image of thick, clearly animal skin, an almost slimy sheen, the quiver of flesh and muscle.

Hands still tightly gripping the handlebars, the father and son lowered their feet from the pedals and stared.

Thick dust swirled beneath the streetlamps. The tremors gradually subsided.

It seemed a subterranean rumbling still growled about them.

Then, quite abruptly, even that rumbling stopped.

It stopped with a slightly unnatural air, almost as

though a tape recording had been suddenly switched off,
but in any case it had ceased, and their surroundings filled
again with crying babies, the smell of dinner cooking,
raucous TV commercials.

Shall we . . . ?

The father asked with his eyes, and his son nodded.

They stopped their bikes at the intersection and
looked ahead.

A scattering of streetlamps threw down hazy light.
Traces of gas and watermain work were everywhere around
them. The road stretched on with its splitting asphalt,
returned to silence.

"Where'd it go?" the son asked.

"Aaah."

The father shook his head.

The two of them were silent for a while.

"Dad, what do you think it was?"

"I don't know."

"I almost thought it was a rhinoceros. It was too big to
be a cow. It looked seven or eight meters long. And if my
eyes weren't fooling me, it was twice as high as this fence.
That would make it three meters, uh-uh, even taller."

"Aaah," said the father again. "I guess a rhino might
get loose from the zoo sometimes. It's not impossible. But
didn't you see two horns on that thing's head?"

"Horns? Yeah, it did look like two horns."

"So it couldn't be a rhinoceros."

"So it was a cow after all? A bull?"

"It must be. You don't see many of them anymore, but
it's my guess a bull got loose from some farm or pasture
near here."

"Yeah."

"Well, if it keeps on like that, there's going to be one
whale of an accident when it meets a truck."

"Yeah."

The father and son looked back down the road. They listened. But aside from the cheerful night noises with their tales of domestic peace and tranquillity, there were no hints of anything amiss in the town.

Almost as though it never happened.

The father shook his head.

If I'd been alone, I'd have thought I was hallucinating.

After a long while the father and son pedaled silently and hurried along the road home. The street began its gradual ascent, and they stopped several times to rest.

The town spread out behind them. They turned and looked back, but there were no signs of anything unusual, no accusing shadows, and nowhere a trembling of the earth, a rising plume of dust.

"Dad, did you see the tail?" the son asked suddenly.

"Mmmm, what about it?"

"Didn't you see it? A superfat tail?"

The father and son reached the crest of the hill and passed through the last sparse copse of trees.

Suddenly their own subdivision lay before them.

The lights were on in all the new houses of the new town, but somehow—perhaps because of the sharp glare of the scattered mercury-vapor lamps—the homes seemed to hunch stockily against the earth.

The mother had dinner ready for them.

"Oh, come on now. Was it really that big?"

Chopsticks in midair, the mother eyed the father and son across the dinner table.

"It was! It was so big I thought it was a rhino."

"Well, it's terrible if it's true. The whole town must be in an uproar."

"Actually there wasn't any at all. Even the running noise stopped, just like that."

"That's right. It stopped like we'd never heard a thing."

"But that's impossible. Oh, I see now. That's why you two were so interested in the news all of a sudden. And did they say anything about it on the news?"

"Not a thing. But it may be too early, too soon, for it to get on the news."

"Boy, it's gotta get on the news! Look, it's seven, eight meters long for sure, and at least three meters high."

"I think you're just exaggerating. Really, have you ever seen or even heard of a cow that big? This isn't a joke, is it? You're not playing games with me?"

"We are not. Anyway, we saw it for sure. Didn't we, Dad?"

"Absolutely. If that was a cow, it'd be a cinch there'd be steaks for five hundred people or more."

"Oh, stop it this instant! You are joking."

The mother laughed shrilly, and the father and son looked at each other, their expressions strangely vague.

After a while the father also laughed, dryly, shortly.

"Well, it hardly matters. There was a little earthquake; then that thing went zipping by. So we got a good shock out of it. Maybe the shadows threw us off, made it look bigger than it was. All that's really certain is that it wasn't a dog or a pig or some animal like that, but a really big rascal, right?"

"Yeah." The son nodded, still not quite satisfied, and began to work his chopsticks.

A variety show was on the television screen. A skimpily clad Eurasian girl was weaving her arms and legs as she sang, almost howled, in a strange, strained voice. The wife laughed shrilly again.

"What is it?"

"The singer, she just blew her nose!"

"Her nose?"

"Oh, come on! You were just telling me about it yesterday, weren't you? You said this girl sometimes blows her nose when she's straining too hard. I thought I'd never heard anything so stupid in my life, but really just now she blew her nose. I, oh, it's too *funny!*"

The mother rolled with laughter again.

The father and son smiled tightly and lowered their eyes.

The father stayed up nearly half that night, drinking. His wife and son had gone to bed, but he, somehow unable to sleep, rose and, putting his legs up to the electric heater in the living room, propped himself up on one arm and began to drink leisurely away at the whiskey he poured little by little into his glass. The last news of the day started on the television, left on since early evening, but, as expected, there was no mention of the shadow they had seen.

Were we really just seeing things?

The alcohol seeped through every cell in his aching muscles, slowly tanning his exhausted body like leather. At least that was how it felt to the father as he continued to watch the shifting screen.

At some point he dozed off.

Someone was blowing his nose. Gradually the noise grew rougher, increasing in violence until it sounded like bellows. *This is no joke. No singer's going to blow her nose like that. This is one heck of a dream.* Half-asleep, half-awake, his mind spun idly.

Eventually the noise was joined by a low moan, shameless and huge, as though echoing from inside a mammoth cave. *No way. This isn't that singer's voice. What's going on?*

His eyes snapped open.

A moan.

A noise like a bellows.

And the sounds continued.

He looked at the television set. The station was already off the air, and the screen held a sandstorm of crackling light. He turned it off and listened.

The noise was coming from outside.

The father peered through a crack in the curtains.

Scraggly potted plants filled the little garden, no larger than a cat's forehead. Beyond the hedge loomed a huge black shadow, with an eye that glittered piercingly in the dark.

It did look a little like a rhinoceros.

But the horn on its nose was even sharper than a rhino's, and beneath it the mouth curved like a raptor's beak, and from that mouth puffed violent white breath like a steam locomotive.

The head was fully a third the size of the body, resembling a buffalo's. Two long horns jutted out like spears, but the turned-up, helmetlike shield between the head and abdomen was like that of no other animal he had ever seen.

A door opened.

The father turned to find his son standing in the room. The boy had pulled his trousers on over his pajamas, and he looked soberly at his father as he pushed one arm into his sweater.

"Is it there?" the son asked in a low voice.

"Yes."

The father jerked his jaw in the direction of the shadow outside.

The mammoth animal scratched the fence twice, three times with the tips of its horns, then slowly swung its side

toward them. It began to walk. Like a heavy tank moving
out for a night battle.

The dark brown back, the hips, the thick, heavy tail
like a giant lizard's trailing down from those hips, all these
passed slowly through their field of vision. The quiver of
muscle beneath thick skin.

"That's not a cow or rhino," said the son, his voice
sticking in his throat.

"It seems to be a dinosaur. That's all I can think of."

"If it's really a dinosaur, then I've seen it in my books.
It's a famous one. Not *Allosaurus*, but *Stegosaurus—*"

"This one's beak is pointed, but its teeth don't look like
much."

"It has a mouth like a beak?"

"That's right."

"Then it's *Triceratops*! Isn't that right, Dad! *Triceratops*. It means the three-horned dinosaur. The nose horn
and two on its forehead, that makes three, right!"

"Then that's it. *Triceratops*."

Triceratops, living and fighting and fighting again in
an endless struggle for survival in the late Cretaceous,
Mesozoic world seventy million years before, domain of
history's most savage beast, the carnivorous monster *Tyrannosaurus rex*. *Triceratops*, that massive herbivore, pos-
sessing the most powerful armament of any animal ever
known. Triceratops, *that* triceratops, was even now walking leisurely down the road before their very eyes.

"Shall we go outside?"

"Sure!"

Father and son slipped through the entrance door of
their home. It was chilly outside, but there was no wind.

Ten meters away the small mountains of triceratops's
hips swayed steadily forward, dragging a tail like a tele-
phone pole. They couldn't see the beast's face beyond the

expansive sweep of the shield. But from triceratops's posture they could well imagine its cautious advance, front legs crouched, head lowered, body in readiness for the slightest sign of danger.

At last triceratops reached the end of the street. Before it stood a stone fence and to the left and right, walls of brick and stone.

He'll head back this way.

Father and son drew back between the gateposts, but in the next instant they stopped, rooted speechless in their tracks.

Triceratops did not stop. It put its head up against the stone wall and sank smoothly into the hard surface. The shield vanished, the front legs and the slice of backbone above them vanished, the hips and hind legs vanished, the tail from base to tip, inch by steady inch, simply disappeared.

Morning came, and the father, setting off to work, and the son, setting off for school, both left the house at the same time.

The father and son exchanged glances and walked to the stone fence at the end of the road. The wall stood solidly, blocking their way.

They fingered it, but found nothing unusual.

Nor was there a single break in the mortar-painted sides, the window glass of the house beyond the wall.

"I've read about dimensional faults and stuff like that," the son said.

"Mmmm. But those are all just theories."

"Theories?"

"When you say that something you can't prove might be this way or that way, that's a theory."

"So there aren't any dimensional faults?"

"Well, someone just thought them up. They might really exist, and they might not. If you figure they exist, then the surface of this wall must be right about the fault line. Between our world and the world of *Triceratops*, seventy million years ago. But really you can try explaining it just about any way you please."

"For instance?"

"For instance, you could think that our world and *Triceratops*'s world exist simultaneously. Instead of popping in and out of a fault line every now and then, we're really both here all the time with just a bit of a lag in between. That would explain why we can somehow look through into that other world, and they can look through to us. It'd be just that fine a difference."

"Huh?"

"I started thinking about it when there was a thick, warm animal smell in the house this morning. And this isn't the first time, you know. It's been like this for at least two or three months now. The people living here must be experiencing the same thing."

"Triceratops went inside their house?"

"You've got it now."

"So can they see it, too? Just like us?"

"Maybe. But you know how people's heads are. We try to deny things that we think are impossible. It's a kind of protective instinct. So even if we somehow do see it, or feel it, we usually just shut it out automatically, choose not to see it, not to do it. If we see it again, two, three times maybe, then common sense comes to the rescue and we laugh it off. 'Nerves.' 'Boy, what a crazy idea!' And that's the end of it."

"And if it still doesn't stop?"

"Then people stop accepting you. You can't live a productive social life anymore."

The boy shook his head lightly from side to side, then
laughed.

"What's so funny?"

"Nothing much. I was just thinking about Mom. I
didn't tell her what I saw last night. Can you guess what
would happen to me if I did?"

The father laughed, too.

"Well, she'd sure put you on the rack. That is, if it
wasn't right after she'd just seen the same thing herself."

"I guess I can't tell any of my friends about it, either."

"Of course not. Now let's get going. We can talk it over
when we get home."

The father and son started walking.

Occasionally speaking and laughing happily together.

And every time they met a neighbor:

"Good morning!"

"Good morning!"

Scattering high-spirited greetings all about them.

The father and son often saw dinosaurs after that.

Sometimes, glancing up at the sunset, they'd glimpse
the shadow of a huge winged creature like *Pteranodon*,
weaving across the sky. But the only earth-hugging dinosaurs they saw were triceratopses.

Apparently the local habitat was best suited to *Triceratops*. The beast asleep in the garage, its head so perfectly
aligned with the family car that it seemed a strange horned
automobile was snoring humorously away, the huge dinosaur passing over the head of a small child crying fretfully
by the roadside, all these apparitions were triceratopses.

Sometimes the father and son would even see them—
though only transparently—walking the sunbathed road in
full daylight.

Nor was it only what they could see. The cloying

animal smell, the low grunting. Running nonstop to the station on ice-stretched, frigid mornings as they gasped and choked on impossible flower pollen. Listening to the distant, bassoonlike cries of a female triceratops in heat, howling through the long night.

You and your dad seem awfully close these days. Anything special going on?

There were days when his mother would badger him, but the son simply grinned.

"Nothing special" was all he'd say.

It was on one of those days, yet another Sunday evening when they had gone cycling about the neighborhood, though not as far as on the day they first met triceratops. After passing through the copse on the top of the hill and coming out above their subdivision, the father and son came to a stop, finding themselves speechless and unable to move.

A triceratops huddled superimposed over every house in the town, their skin—brilliant green beneath the mercury lamps—gently rising and falling with their breathing. Occasionally one would open its eyes in a narrow slit, and every time the lids raised, the pupils would glitter in brilliant rose, perhaps because of rhodopsin pigment like that found in some species of crocodile.

It was a scene of phantasmal beauty, like the winking of giant fireflies.

"Do you suppose the land over there's the same as the town?"

"Maybe they can see us and feel us like we feel them. Maybe they're just trying to keep warm."

"You may be right."

"Isn't it a weird feeling? Everyone's going to work or leaving for school from a dinosaur's belly, and they're coming home to the belly, eating dinner, watching TV."

"But that's how it is."

"Hey, my room's in its butt."

"Don't let it get to you."

"But it's really peaceful somehow, isn't it? They may look fierce, but I've never seen a triceratops fighting."

"They hardly ever run, either."

"Yeah, that's right. Just the one we saw that first time, in the other town."

"I wonder what he was running for."

"Anyway, it's peaceful enough today."

"There's nothing better than peace."

The peace did not last long.

It was a day when yellow sand blown from the continent filled the air and turned the sun the color of blood, a harsh, unpleasant day.

It was the day that the son, looking casually toward the national highway from the hilltop while returning from a friend's house, saw a dozen dinosaurs running on strange hind legs—like ostriches—long tails held high, kicking up clouds of dust.

"Those were tyrannosauruses for sure. Superfat back legs and little skinny front ones like decorations. Pointed mouths. Anyway, tyrannosauruses. And they were really moving fast. They came running at least as far as the station."

"We're just a little way from the station here, but I didn't feel anything like tyrannosaurus when I was coming home just now. Even the triceratops in the garage just opened his eyes a bit and stared at me like he always does."

"But I really did see them."

"Maybe they ran right through town and went somewhere else?"

"But I wonder why they would do that. They went out of sight near the station."

"Hmmm."

The father crossed his arms.

"In that case maybe they're still milling around there somewhere. Or maybe—"

"Let's go see," said the son.

"You two are up to something again, aren't you?"

The mother shouted after them. The father and son smiled, waved, and mounted their bicycles.

They went as far as the station, but there was no trace of any tyrannosauruses. After watching the station plaza for a while, they turned leisurely back home.

A small creek flowed close to the station, completely covered with concrete. There was a playground built on top of it. The long, covered drain formed a second road, stretching almost to their subdivision.

"Let's go back this way."

The father and son pedaled their bicycles slowly over the concrete plating. The tires bounced heavily every time they jumped a gap between the plates.

Their front lights waved widely.

Before long they became aware of a strange noise. It sounded like rapid water and, an octave lower, the grunting of countless pigs. Moments later they felt the earth begin to rumble.

And suddenly they looked down at their feet. And ran to the metal lid of an air vent.

They were running beneath the metal mesh of the lid, fiercely kicking up the water as they ran. Their wet hides glistened; their necks were outstretched. The pack of tyrannosauruses dashed for the subdivision like a conveyor belt, a never-ending stream.

They had been following the water-course. The group

near the national highway had been but a single part, a
flying column, and had merged with the main group at the
station.

"This is bad."

It hardly mattered if they hurried, yet the father and
son began to pedal furiously.

As they neared the subdivision, countless tyrannosauruses danced up through the concrete sheeting ahead of
them, looking like a geyser of muddy water.

All the houses on the slanting slope of the subdivision
heaved up their roofs and began to move.

The triceratops had risen.

The fighting began.

Before their eyes, a triceratops, head lowered,
charged toward and plunged sharp horns into the carotid
artery of an attacking tyrannosaurus. The carnivore, its
blood fountaining into the air like water from a fire hose,
fell back, lashed its long tail, and leaped hugely, gouging
out the triceratop's eyes with a single sweep of the
key-shaped claws on its forelegs.

Three more tyrannosauruses swooped onto the mammoth body of the triceratops, crumpled just six meters in
front of their home. The huge reptiles plunged razor teeth
into the belly meat, already ripped apart by their claws.
The surroundings were flooded in a murky river of blood.

"Isn't that our triceratops?" cried the boy, his voice
shaking.

"You're right."

A tyrannosaurus had fallen in front of the entranceway.
The father and son warily watched its huge bloodshot eyes,
the convulsive contractions of its belly, as they wheeled
their bikes up the driveway.

The fighting lasted throughout the night.

Even at the height of the raucous laughter of a

televised singing contest, the father and son could hear the war cries, could feel the thick hide splitting, the shrieks of the hour of death.

By morning the combat had almost ended, and the countless corpses of triceratops and tyrannosauruses, some still barely twitching the tips of their tails, some dragging the ripped tatters of their stomachs, lay tumbled across the landscape.

Almost without exception, the corpses of triceratops had their entrails dug out, their ribs laid bare, and their neck shields chopped into ribbons. But most of the tyrannosauruses showed only deep puncture wounds in their necks and bellies, escaping utter destruction.

There were even a few scattered survivors. But none had escaped unscathed. All had lost the energy to keep on fighting.

One tyrannosaurus, his flung-out leg half mincemeat from the thigh down, continued to drag out and gobble the guts of the triceratops he had slaughtered.

Behind him sprawled the body of one of his comrades, a gaping hole bored through its neck, its body clotted with dried blood, while no more than five meters away a triceratops grazed silently on the grass, blood still seeping from one of its eyes.

Every now and then the tyrannosaurus would raise its head and glare—though perhaps this was only their fancy—balefully at the grazing triceratops.

If you eat that crud, why'd you kill us?

The father and son almost felt they could hear that voice.

If there's too much to eat, why did you keep on butchering us?

The triceratop's unbloodied eye seemed to ask that back.

The father and son watched as they walked slowly to the station. The corpses that weren't dripping were at least tolerable. But even they were brought up short where the large intestines of a tyrannosaurus lay heaped across the road, as if they had sprung writhing from the animal's torn-open belly. After a moment's pause they edged by on the side of the street.

A woman in fashionable white slacks passed through that blood-smeared landscape, her shoes clicking loudly, her eyes suspiciously watching father and son.

A microbus filled with kindergarteners passed through that landscape, bearing its load of lively chatter.

An elementary-school student passed through that landscape, singing a jingle.

Skylark dancing to the sky.

God is reigning in the sky.

The world, the world's a trifle.

TAKU MAYUMURA

FNIFMUM

Translated by
Katsumi Shindo and Grania Davis

A surreal love story that spans centuries.

Awakening from sleep, Fnifmum stayed in a haze for awhile.

All he could see were rocks and the sea, because his sensory organ wasn't activated yet. The mounds of black rocks weren't rocking in the gale, and the waves in the sea weren't waving at all. He could see some white wave-crests offshore, where the wind must be especially strong, but they were motionless too. There was no keening of the wind. It was a soundless world.

This was natural because his sensory organ was closed, so he couldn't perceive any movement. His sensory organ seemed to move unconsciously to this monotonous time-point while he was sleeping.

Recovering control, Fnifmum moved his awakening sensory organ toward the past end of his body. He decided to watch the furious battle between the races of Pultera and Cakyo in the distant past, which was located on his tail.

His sensory organ was gaining speed, and he saw the two suns and three moons in the sky become belts of different colors. Before they merged and surrounded him in a sparkling gray chaos, Fnifmum cut his eyesight. He'd seen this before, and he didn't like to repeat the same scenery.

His other senses told him that he was still going backward into the past.

Shall I stop here? I think I could see the most exciting scene from this time-point, excluding the smaller battles that came before.

And he was right.

Numberless lights glittered and darted through the night sky. Now the two huge space battalions were approaching each other.

Fnifmum allowed his sensory organ to float on the time-stream, and watched.

The vast armies of light passed alongside each other, and shooting their terrible beams. Thousands of sparkling colors exploded.

After watching this climax, Fnifmum sent his sensory organ to the start of the battle, and altered his sensitivity to electro-magnetic waves.

Then the image of the battle changed. Each light was

covered with an oval of pale color and radiating lines of varied hues. As the battle proceeded, the opposing lights exploded gorgeously, one after another.

After watching the spectacle in various styles, he closed his sensory organ.

He knew what would happen next. The Pultera would win the battle and would advance towards Fnifmum. They would construct their base, which would last for several ages. Eventually another army of Cakyo would come to wage war against the base. A violent battle would break out, and both armies would be destroyed by powerful bombs. Then no more Pultera would appear.

Fnifmum had observed this process twice, and discovered that Pultera and Cakyo were the names of the two races that fought in the night sky.

But he wouldn't watch the entire process again this time. He wasn't interested since he had seen it twice before. Besides, his body ached at the time-point of the explosion of the final bomb. If the bomb had been just a little more powerful, his body might have been cut at this time-point. It was such an awful explosion.

Gazing at the halted battle scene, he wondered where he should go. He hadn't visited every time-point along his body. There must be so many pleasant time-points waiting to be found—finding them was what gave him vitality.

Then he recalled Honycominah.

His body had some physical contacts with others of his phylum at various time-points. When his sensory organ contacted another and found it congenial, they exchanged genes stored in their sensory organs, through the surface of their bodies. The received genes would be dropped at another time-point and disappear. Actually they wouldn't disappear, but would grow into a branching time-line as his child—but there was no contact. Fnifmum lay in his own time-line and knew nothing outside it.

He sometimes wondered why the gene exchanges couldn't be known in advance. But the progress of time inside his body wasn't flexible like external time, which proceeds naturally. He could understand this fact, but couldn't comprehend much beyond it.

His contact with Honycominah was at the oldest time-point of all the contacts with his phylum. He had often exchanged genes with Honycominah. Her body seemed to be moving farther away spatially, as they both grew in time away from the point of contact. So they usually exchanged news that they couldn't find in their own time-lines. This was uncommon for their phylum, but he and Honycominah were especially congenial.

He decided to visit Honycominah. If Honycominah's sensory organ wasn't there, he would wait awhile for it. He sent his sensory organ from the sky battle of the two races to the far past.

He was confused when his sensory organ reached the end of his tail. He couldn't find the contact-point with Honycominah. His sensory organ couldn't reach far enough into the past to make contact.

This meant one thing certain for Fnifmum; he had grown past the time-point.

He had been growing from the time he had been conscious of himself. First he was just a little boy of five to ten years. Now he was two thousand years long. The growth didn't occur at both ends of his body. He was influenced by the effects of time, though Fnifmum was a creature who lay outside time. His body grew toward the future, while the past end of his body shrank closer and closer to the future end. The difference between this expanding and contracting of his body was his total growth.

If his vital energy diminished, his growth toward the future would slow. Then the length of his body would decrease as the past end shrank toward the future end. Eventually both body and mind would shrink away. Fnifmum knew this from instinct and from the tales of his phylum.

Because of the contracting of his past end, he could no longer send his sensory organ to the contact point with Honycominah. His body had passed beyond Honycominah, who had a younger body of only around five hundred years. No doubt that he had left the contact time-point behind.

Fnifmum had anticipated that this day would come, but when it actually happened he felt a great emptiness. He had lost many contacts with his phylum before, but Honycominah was his most valuable companion.

Fnifmum knew this situation from his experiences when some of his phylum has passed beyond him. The time-line which had the contact with Honycominah still remained, but it was now an inorganic point which his sensory organ could no longer reach. The image of his dying body linked to his live body made Fnifmum feel very depressed, as though he could no longer control his sensory organ.

Yet there was nothing to do. Whatever he thought or understood, it was clear that he could no longer talk with Honycominah. It was as if Honycominah no longer existed for him, or so he thought.

Reluctantly, Fnifmum stopped thinking.

He felt rather dull. If he didn't move his sensory organ and stayed there, he would fall asleep. He didn't care. It was all the same to him . . . It didn't make any difference at all.

Then Fnifmum realized something. After the last

sleep he had lost contact with Honycominah. His tail had
passed her by. That meant he had slept a long time. While
he slept, the past end of his body moved up the time-line.
That meant the future end should have grown toward the
future.

He could find out whether he was still growing, or
shrinking after his life's zenith, if he explored the future
end of his body. The instinct of all living things captured
him, and he moved his sensory organ hesitantly toward the
future, with some hope and a lot of anxiety.

He slowly approached the future end that he had
known before. If his body came to a stop there, then all he
could do was wait for his end to come.

Tensely he continued to move his sensory organ.

It passed beyond the time-point that he remembered
as the farthest future end.

Feeling relieved, Fnifmum moved carefully to the
further future. It went beyond what he'd expected. He
found that he had grown far more than he had lost on his
past end. He had been growing steadily, not losing power
as he had feared.

Sending his sensory organ outward, he saw something
unfamiliar moving outside. He slowed down and floated on
the natural time-stream.

Something bright was approaching in the sky, where
two suns were shining. It moved rapidly and came down
near Fnifmum. It was a small space ship.

The outside of its hull was seriously damaged. There
were several large holes on its surface, the paint was
peeling off, and some melted things clung here and there.
A square panel on the surface slid aside, and two creatures
emerged.

This was the first time he'd seen such figures. They

had transparent balls on top of each body. Inside was something rather round, with odd projections and holes.

The transparent ball was supported by a column. A pair of limbs extended from the upper portion, and a larger pair of limbs supported the lower part of the column. The upper limbs seemed to be used for manufacturing, and the lower limbs for moving.

The two creatures put the bottoms of their columns directly on the ground for a while, alongside their space ship. Then they drew near each other.

Gradually Fnifmum became aware of their communication, though it was weak and flickering, and he could barely understand such faltering mentalities. One of them suddenly radiated a strong thought-process.

"Just as I thought, it's impossible to breathe on this planet. It's all over now. Hopeless."

"Courage, sweet organ." One of them held out a limb to pat the other's column. "We'll find a way. We must!"

"But our ship is damaged, and our air supply in the tanks is only good for around thirty minutes."

"Dear one, use your imagination."

"For what? We have no hope now. It's too late to call the Space Troop Rescue Team. Besides, it's better to suffocate here than be destroyed by the Space Troop."

Their mentalities were vague for awhile. Then Fnifmum became aware of ten bright spots streaking through the sky.

"There they come!" Suddenly one of them stood up upon the lower limbs. "Scouts from the Space Troop! They must have followed our ship."

But the other one didn't reply. He was manipulating a mechanical item on his upper limb.

"What are you doing?" Her mentality communicated

powerfully, "Sweet-organ, what's the matter with you . . .
the scouts are coming!"

The bright spots grew larger and larger.

"The time mechanism . . ."

Holding the small object up, he rose quickly. "Use the
emergency escape time-mechanism!"

"It's no use! Any time-point we go they can follow and
find us easily. Where could we go with the time-
mechanism? We have so little air supply."

"There's just a slight possibility." Moving toward the
damaged ship, he explained, "The air contains so much
carbonic acid gas—and there's a sea over there. So . . ."

She answered with a more cheerful mentality. "Right!
Perhaps plants will appear here—or they already exist—
and propagate themselves. Then they might create enough
oxygen for us to breathe."

He went to the space ship and brought back a complex
device. They collaborated to set it along Fnifmum's time-
space.

"Better to destroy the ship so they'll think we're
dead."

As she spoke, he took some kind of weapon from his
belt and shot a pulsing light-beam at the ship, which
instantly flared and collapsed into a pile of debris.

"Let's go—as far into the future as we can!"

Her mentality communicated to his. He nodded,
astride the device with her. Then he picked up a little
mechanism, which he had dropped.

"Almost forgot to take this. Without it we can't know if
the air is breathable."

Her mentality communicated to his with soft warmth.
Fnifmum watched them communicate by touching and
embracing delicately.

"There are only the two of us," she thought.

He held her with his upper limbs. "We're together whether we live or die."

They turned a switch to start the device and rode upon it together.

"To the farthest future we can go!"

Then Fnifmum discovered that they lay within the same time-stream that he did. They were inside his own time-line, alongside his body. He experienced a novel, sympathetic feeling.

This made a strong impression on Fnifmum. He couldn't tell whether the feeling came from the new empathetic emotion, or from watching the two creatures embracing each other—it didn't matter.

He was captivated by the good feeling, which was different from the one he felt when he exchanged genes with Honycominah.

He wanted to know how they would be, so he sent his sensory organ into the future, faster than the speed of the natural time-stream. But at last he had to stop.

Though they lay alongside him, farther into the future, he couldn't move his sensory organ beyond the future end of his body. There was nothing he could do.

To grow, Fnifmum thought. If he grew he could see them in the future. He must keep growing until he found out how they would be. Fortunately, he's still growing. Perhaps he can grow far enough into the future to reach them.

All he can do is wait. He must wait patiently.

Fnifmum moved his sensory organ and observed the scene with the two creatures one more time.

Then he fell asleep.

YASUTAKA TSUTSUI

STANDING WOMAN

Translated by David Lewis

A future society uses a frightening method to provide urban greenery.

I stayed up all night and finally finished a forty-page short story. It was a trivial entertainment piece, capable of neither harm nor good.

"These days you can't write stories that might do harm or good: it can't be helped." That's what I told myself while I fastened the manuscript with a paper clip and put it into an envelope.

As to whether I have it in me to write stories that

might do harm or good, I do my best not to think about it.
I might want to try.

The morning sunlight hurt my eyes as I slipped on my
wooden clogs and left the house with the envelope. Since
there was still time before the first mail truck would come,
I turned my feet toward the park. In the morning no
children come to this park, a mere eighty square meters in
the middle of a cramped residential district. It's quiet here.
So I always include the park in my morning walk. Nowadays even the scanty green provided by the ten or so trees
is priceless in the megalopolis.

I should have brought some bread, I thought. My
favorite dogpillar stands next to the park bench. It's an
affable dogpillar with buff-colored fur, quite large for a
mongrel.

The liquid-fertilizer truck had just left when I reached
the park; the ground was damp and there was a faint smell
of chlorine. The elderly gentleman I often saw there was
sitting on the bench next to the dogpillar, feeding the buff
post what seemed to be meat dumplings. Dogpillars usually have excellent appetites. Maybe the liquid fertilizer,
absorbed by the roots sunk deep in the ground and passed
on up through the legs, leaves something to be desired.

They'll eat just about anything you give them.

"You brought him something? I slipped up today. I
forgot to bring my bread," I said to the elderly man.

He turned gentle eyes on me and smiled softly.

"Ah, you like this fellow, too?"

"Yes," I replied sitting down beside him. "He looks
exactly like the dog I use to have."

The dogpillar looked up at me with large, black eyes
and wagged its tail.

"Actually, I kept a dog like this fellow myself," the man
said, scratching the ruff of the dogpillar's neck. "He was

made into a dogpillar when he was three. Haven't you seen
him? Between the haberdashery and the film shop on the
coast road. Isn't there a dogpillar there that looks like this
fellow?"

I nodded, adding, "Then that one was yours?"

"Yes, he was our pet. His name was Hachi. Now he's
completely vegetized. A beautiful dogtree."

"Now that you mention it, he does look a lot like this
fellow. Maybe they came from the same stock."

"And the dog you kept?" the elderly man asked.
"Where is he planted?"

"Our dog was named Buff," I answered, shaking my
head. "He was planted beside the entrance to the cemetery
on the edge of town when he was four. Poor thing, he died
right after he was planted. The fertilizer trucks don't get
out that way very often, and it was so far I couldn't take him
food every day. Maybe they planted him badly. He died
before becoming a tree."

"Then he was removed?"

"No, fortunately, it didn't much matter there if he
smelled or not, and so he was left there and dried. Now
he's a bonepillar. He makes fine material for the neighborhood elementary-school science class, I hear."

"That's wonderful."

The elderly man stroked the dogpillar's head. "This
fellow here, I wonder what he was called before he became
a dogpillar."

"No calling a dogpillar by its original name," I said.
"Isn't that a strange law?"

The man looked at me sharply, then replied casually,
"Didn't they just extend the laws concerning people to
dogs? That's why they lose their names when they become
dogpillars." He nodded while scratching the dogpillar's
jaw. "Not only the old names, but you can't give them new

names, either. That's because there are no proper nouns for plants."

Why, of course, I thought.

He looked at my envelope with MANUSCRIPT ENCLOSED written on it.

"Excuse me," he said. "Are you a writer?"

I was a little embarrassed.

"Well, yes. Just trivial things."

After looking at me closely, the man returned to stroking the dogpillar's head. "I also use to write things."

He managed to suppress a smile.

"How many years is it now since I stopped writing? It feels like a long time."

I stared at the man's profile. Now that he said so, it was a face I seemed to have seen somewhere before. I started to ask his name, hesitated, and fell silent.

The elderly man said abruptly. "It's become a hard world to write in."

I lowered my eyes, ashamed of myself, who still continued to write in such a world.

The man apologized flurriedly at my sudden depression.

"That was rude. I'm not criticizing you. I'm the one who should feel ashamed."

"No," I told him, after looking quickly around us, "I can't give up writing, because I haven't the courage. Giving up writing! Why, after all, that would be a gesture against society."

The elderly man continued stroking the dogpillar. After a long while he spoke.

"It's painful, suddenly giving up writing. Now that it's come to this, I would have been better off if I'd gone on boldly writing social criticism and had been arrested. There are even times when I think that. But I was just a dilettante, never knowing poverty, craving peaceful dreams. I wanted to live a comfortable life. As a person strong in self-respect, I couldn't endure being exposed to the eyes of the world, ridiculed. So I quit writing. A sorry tale."

He smiled and shook his head. "No, no, let's not talk about it. You never know who might be listening, even here on the street."

I changed the subject. "Do you live here?"

"Do you know the beauty parlor on the main street? You turn in there. My name is Hiyama." He nodded at me. "Come over sometime. I'm married, but. . . ."

"Thank you very much."

I gave him my own name.

I didn't remember any writer named Hiyama. No doubt he wrote under a pen name. I had no intention of visiting his house. This is a world where even two or three writers getting together is considered illegal assembly.

"It's time for a mail truck to come in."

Taking pains to look at my watch, I stood.

"I'm afraid I'd better go." I said.

He turned a sadly smiling face toward me and bowed slightly. After stroking the dogpillar's head a little, I left the park.

I came out on the main street, but there was only a ridiculous number of passing cars: pedestrians were few. A cattree, about thirty to forty centimeters high, was planted next to the sidewalk.

Sometimes I come across a catpillar that has just been planted and still hasn't become a cattree. New catpillars look at my face and meow or cry, but the ones where all four limbs planted in the ground have vegetized, with their greenish faces stiffly set and eyes shut tight, only move their ears now and then. Then there are catpillars that grow branches from their bodies and put out handfuls of leaves. The mental condition of these seems to be completely vegetized—they don't even move their ears. Even if a cat's face can still be made out, it may be better to call these cattrees.

Maybe, I thought, it's better to make dogs into dog-pillars. When their food runs out, they get vicious and even turn on people. But why did they have to turn cats into catpillars? Too many strays? To improve the food situation by even a little? Or perhaps for the greening of the city. . . .

Next to the big hospital on the corner where the highways intersect are two mantrees, and ranged alongside these trees is a manpillar. This manpillar wears a postman's uniform, and you can't tell how far its legs have vegetized because of its trousers. It is male, thirty-five of thirty-six years old, tall, with a bit of a stoop.

I approached him and held out my envelope as always.

"Registered mail, special delivery, please."

The manpillar, nodding silently, accepted the envelope and took stamps and a registered-mail slip from his pocket.

I looked around quickly after paying the postage. There was no one else there. I decided to try speaking to him. I gave him mail every three days, but I still hadn't had a chance for a leisurely talk.

"What did you do?" I asked in a low voice .

The manpillar looked at me surprise. Then, after running his eyes around the area, he answered with a sour look, "Won't do to go saying unnecessary things to me. Even me, I'm not supposed to answer."

"I know that," I said, looking into his eyes.

When I wouldn't leave, he took a deep breath. "I just said the pay's low. What's more, I got heard by my boss.

Because a postman's pay is really low." With a dark look, he jerked his jaw at the two mantrees next to him. "These guys were the same. Just for letting slip some complaints about low pay. Do you know them?" he asked me.

I pointed at one of the mantrees. "I remember this one, because I gave him a lot of mail. I don't know the other one. He was already a mantree when we moved here."

"That one was my friend," he said.

"Wasn't that other one a chief clerk or section head?"

He nodded. "That's right. Chief clerk."

"Don't you get hungry or cold?"

"You don't feel it that much," he replied, still expressionless. Anyone who's made into a manpillar soon becomes expressionless. "Even I think I've gotten pretty plantlike. Not only in how I feel things, but in the way I think, too. At first, I was sad, but now it doesn't matter. I used to get really hungry, but they say the vegetizing goes faster when you don't eat."

He stared at me with lightless eyes. He was probably hoping he could become a mantree soon.

"Talk says they give people with radical ideas a lobotomy before making them into manpillars, but I didn't get that done, either. Even so a month after I was planted here I didn't get angry anymore."

He glanced at my wristwatch. "Well, you better go now. It's almost time for the mail truck to come."

"Yes," But still I couldn't leave, and I hesitated uneasily.

"You," the manpillar said. "Someone you know didn't recently get done into a manpillar, did they?"

Cut to the quick. I stared at his face for a moment, then nodded slowly.

"Actually, my wife."

"Hmm, your wife, is it?" For a few moments he regarded me with deep interest. "I wondered whether it wasn't something like that. Otherwise nobody ever bothers to talk to me. Then what did she do, your wife?"

"She complained that prices were high at a house-wives' get-together. Had that been all, fine, but she criticized the government, too. I'm starting to make it big as a writer, and I think that the eagerness of being that writer's wife made her say it. One of the women there informed on her. She was planted on the left side of the road looking from the station toward the assembly hall and next to that hardware store."

"Ah, that place." He closed his eyes a little, as if recollecting the appearance of the buildings and the stores in that area. "It's a fairly peaceful street. Isn't that for the better?" He opened his eyes and looked at me searchingly. "You aren't going to see her, are you? It's better not to see her to often. Both for her and you. That way you both forget faster."

"I know that."

I hung my head.

"Your wife?" he asked, his voice turning slightly sympathetic. "Has anyone done anything to her?"

"No. So far nothing. She's just standing, but even so—"

"Hey," The manpillar serving as a postbox raised his jaw to attract my attention. "It's come. The mail truck. You'd better go."

"You're right."

Taking a few wavering steps, as if pushed by his voice, I stopped and looked back. "Isn't there anything you want done?"

He brought a hard smile to his cheeks and shook his head.

The red mail truck stopped beside him.
I moved on past the hospital.

Thinking I'd check in on my favorite bookstore. I
entered a street of crowded shops. My new book was
suppose to be out any day now, but that kind of thing no
longer made me the slightest bit happy.

A little before the bookstore in the same row is a small,
cheap, candy store, and on the edge of the road in front of
it is a manpillar on the verge of becoming a mantree. A
young male, it is already a year since it was planted. The
face had become a brownish color tinged with green, and
the eyes are tightly shut. Tall back slightly bent, the
posture slouching a little forward. The legs, torso, and
arms, visible through clothes reduced to rags by exposure
to wind and rain, are already vegetized, and here and there
branches sprout. Young leaves bud from the ends of
the arms, raised above the shoulders like beating wings.
The body, which has become a tree, and even the face no
longer move at all. The heart has sunk into the tranquil
world of plants.

I imagined the day when my wife would reach this
state, and again my heart winced with pain, trying to
forget. It was the anguish of trying to forget.

If I turn the corner at this candy store and go straight,
I thought. *I can go to where my wife is standing. I can see
my wife. But it won't do to go,* I told myself. *There's no
telling who might see you: if the woman who informed on
her questioned you, you'd really be in trouble.* I came to a
halt in front of the candy store and peered down the road.
Pedestrian traffic was the same as always. *It's all right.
Anyone would overlook it if you just stand and talk a bit.
You'll just have a word or two.* Defying my own voice
screaming, *"Don't go!"* I went briskly down the street.

Her face pale, my wife was standing by the road in front of the hardware store. Her legs were unchanged, and it only seemed as if her feet from the ankles down were buried in the earth. Expressionlessly, as if striving to see nothing, feel nothing, she stared steadily ahead. Compared with two days before, her cheeks seemed a bit hollow. Two passing factory workers pointed at her, made some vulgar joke, and passed on, guffawing uproariously. I went up to her and raised my voice.

"Michiko!" I yelled right in her ear.

My wife looked at me, and blood rushed to her cheeks. She brushed one hand through her tangled hair.

"You've come again? Really you mustn't."

"I can't help coming."

The hardware-store mistress, tending shop, saw me. With an air of feigned indifference, she averted her eyes and retired to the back of the store. Full of gratitude for her consideration, I drew a few steps closer to Michiko and faced her.

"You've gotten pretty used to it?"

With all her might she formed a bright smile on her stiffened face. "Mmm. I'm used to it."

"Last night it rained a little."

Still gazing at me with large, dark eyes, she nodded lightly. "Please don't worry. I hardly feel anything."

"When I think about you, I can't sleep." I hung my head. "You're always standing out here. When I think that, I can't possibly sleep. Last night I even thought I should bring you an umbrella."

"Please don't do anything like that!" My wife frowned just a little. "It would be terrible if you did something like that."

A large truck drove past behind me. White dust thinly

veiled my wife's hair and shoulders, but she didn't seem bothered.

"Standing isn't really all that bad." She spoke with deliberate lightness, working to keep me from worrying.

I perceived a subtle change in my wife's expressions and speech from two days before. It seemed that her words had lost a shade of delicacy, and the range of her emotions had become somewhat impoverished. *Watching from the sidelines like this, seeing her gradually grow more expressionless, it's all the more desolating for having known her as she was before—those keen responses, the bright vivacity, the rich, full expressions.*

"These people," I asked her, running my eyes over the hardware store, "are they good to you?"

"Well, of course. They're kind at heart. Just once they told me to ask if there's anything I want done. But they still haven't done anything for me."

"Don't you get hungry?"

She shook her head.

"It's better not to eat."

So. Unable to endure being a manpillar, she was hoping to become a mantree even so much as a single day faster.

"So please don't bring me food." She stared at me. "Please forget about me. I think, certainly, even without making any particular effort, I'm going to forget about you. I'm happy that you come to see me, but then the sadness drags on that much longer. For both of us."

"Of course you're right, but—" Despising this self that could do nothing for his own wife, I hung my head again. "But I won't forget you." I nodded. The tears came. "I won't forget. Ever."

When I raised my head and looked at her again, she was gazing steadily at me with eyes that had lost a little of their luster, her whole face beaming in a faint smile like a carved image of Buddha. It was the first time I had ever seen her smile like that.

I felt I was having a nightmare. *No,* I told myself, *This isn't your wife anymore.*

The suit she had been wearing when she was arrested had become terribly dirty and filled with wrinkles. But of course I wouldn't be allowed to bring a change of clothes. My eyes rested on a dark stain on her skirt.

"Is that blood? What happened?"

"Oh, this," she spoke falteringly, looking down at her skirt with a confused air. "Last night two drunks played a prank on me."

"The bastards!" I felt a furious rage at their inhumanity. If you put it to them, they would say that since my wife was no longer human, it didn't matter what they did.

"They can't do that kind of thing! It's against the law!"

"That's right. But I can hardly appeal."

And of course I couldn't go to the police and appeal, either. If I did, I'd be looked on as even more of a problem person.

"The bastards! What did they—" I bit my lip. My heart hurt enough to break. "Did it bleed a lot?"

"Mmm, a little."

"Does it hurt?"

"It doesn't hurt anymore."

Michiko, who had been so proud before now, showed just a little sadness in her face. I was shocked by the change in her. A group of young men and women, penetratingly comparing me and my wife, passed behind me.

"You'll be seen," my wife said anxiously. "I beg of you, don't throw yourself away."

"Don't worry." I smiled thinly for her in self-contempt. "I don't have the courage."

"You should go now."

"When you're a mantree," I said in parting, "I'll peti-
tion. I'll get them to transplant you to our garden."

"Can you do that?"

"I should be able to. " I nodded liberally. "I should be
able to."

"I'd be happy if you could," my wife said expressionlessly.

"Well, see you later."

"It'd be better if you didn't come again," she said in a
murmur, looking down.

"I know. That's my intention. But I'll probably come
anyway."

For a few minutes we were silent.

Then my wife spoke abruptly.

"Goodbye."

"Umm."

I began walking.

When I looked back as I rounded the corner, Michiko
was following me with her eyes, still smiling like a graven
Buddha.

Embracing a heart that seemed ready to split apart, I
walked. I noticed suddenly that I had come out in front of
the station. Unconsciously, I had returned to my usual
walking course.

Opposite the station is a small coffee shop I always go
to called Punch. I went in and sat down in a corner booth.
I ordered coffee, drinking it black. Until then I had always
had it with sugar. The bitterness of sugarless, creamless
coffee pierced my body, and I savored it masochistically.
From now on I'll always drink it black. That was what I
resolved.

Three students in the next booth were talking about a

critic, who had just been arrested and made into a manpillar.

"I hear he was planted smack in the middle of the Ginza."

"He loved the country. He always lived in the country. That's why they set him up in a place like that."

"Seems they gave him a lobotomy."

"And the students who tried to use force in the Diet, protesting his arrest—they've all been arrested and will be made into manpillars, too."

"Weren't there almost thirty of them? Where'll they plant them all?"

"They say they'll be planted in front of their own university, down both sides of a street called Students Road."

"They'll have to change the name now. Violence Grove, or something."

The three snickered.

"Hey, let's not talk about it. We don't want someone to hear."

The three shut up.

When I left the coffee shop and headed home, I realized that I had begun to feel as if I was already a manpillar myself. Murmuring the words of a popular song to myself, I walked on.

I am a wayside manpillar. You, too, are a wayside manpillar. What the hell, the two of us, in this world. Dried grasses that never flower.

TETSU YANO

THE LEGEND OF THE PAPER SPACESHIP

Translated by
Gene Van Troyer and Tomoko Oshiro

*A poignant tale from the dean
of Japanese SF writers.*

*Halfway through the Pacific War, I was sent from my
unit to a village in the heart of the mountains, and there I
lived for some months. I still recall clearly the road leading
into that village; and in the grove of bamboo trees beside
the road, the endless flight of a paper airplane and a
beautiful naked woman running after it. Now, long years
later, I cannot shake the feeling that what she was always
folding out of paper stood for no earthly airplane, but for*

a spaceship. Some time long ago, deep in those mountains recesses . . .

1

The paper airplane glides gracefully above the earth; and weaving between the sprouts of new bamboo, stealing over the deep-piled humus of fallen and decaying leaves, a white mist comes blowing, eddying and dancing up high on the back of a subtle breeze, moving on and on.

In the bamboo grove the flowing mist gathers in thick and brooding pools. Twilight comes quickly to this mountain valley. Like a ship sailing a sea of clouds, the paper airplane flies on and on through the mist.

> *One—a stone stairway to the sky*
> *Two—if it doesn't fly*
> *Three—if it does fly, open . . .*

A woman's voice, singing through the mist. As if pushed onward by that voice, the paper airplane lifts in never-ending flight. A naked woman owns the voice, and white in her nudity she slips quickly between the swaying bamboo of the grove.

(Kill them! Kill them!)

Alarm sirens wove screaming patterns around shrieking voices.

(Kill everyone! That's an order!)

(Don't let any get to the ship! One's escaped!)

(Beamers! Fire, fire!)

A crowd of voices resounding in this mist, but no one else can hear them. These voices echo only in the woman's head.

Tall and leafy and standing like images of charcoal gray

against a pale ash background, the bamboo trees appear
and disappear and reappear among the gauzy veils of the
always folding rolling mist. The fallen leaves whisper as the
woman's feet rustle over them. Mist streams around her
like something alive as she walks, then flows apart before
her to allow the dim shape of what might be a small lake to
peek through.

Endworld Mere: the *uba-iri-no-numa*. After they had
laughed and danced through the promises and passions of
living youth, old people once came often to this place to
end misery of their old age by throwing themselves into the
swamp's murky waters.

Superstition holds that Endworld Mere swarms with
the spirits of the dead. To placate any of the lingering dead,
therefore, these valley folk had heaped numerous mounds
of stones in a small open space near the mere. This place
they named the *Sai no Kawara*, the earthly shore where
the journey over the Great Waters began. They gathered
here once a year for memorial services, when they burnt
incense and clapped hands and sent their prayers across the
Wide Waters to the shore of the nether world.

No matter how many stone towers you erect on the
earthly shore of the River of Three Crossings, the myths
tell us that demons will destroy them. Whether physical or
spectral, here too the "demons" had been about the tireless
task of destruction. In the very beginning there had
probably been but a few mounds of tombstones to conse-
crate the unknown dead; but over the years, hundreds of
stones had been heaped, and now lay scattered. Throughout most of the year, the place was now little more than a
last rest stop where the infrequent person bound on the
one-way trip to Endworld Mere paused for a short time
before moving on. Because of its deserted silence, men and

women seeking a little more excitement in life found the place ideal for secret rendezvous.

Secret meetings were often a singular concern for these simple village folk. They could think of little else but pleasure. "Endworld Mere" is a name that suggests even the old go there with stealth, and possibly the dreadful legends surrounding the place were fabricated by anxious lovers who wished to make it a place more secure for their trystings.

Owing to these frightening stories, the village children gave the mere a wide berth. Round lichen-covered stones, rain-soaked and rotting paper dolls, creaking wooden signs with mysterious, indecipherable characters inscribed on them: For children these things all bespoke the presence of ghosts and ogres and nightmare encounters with demons.

Sometimes, however, the children would unintentionally come close enough to glimpse the dank mere, and on one such occasion they were chasing the madwoman Osen, who was flying a paper airplane.

"Say, guys! Osen's still runnin' aroun' naked!"

"*Hey*, Osen! Doncha wan' any *clothes?*"

All the children jeered Osen. For adult and child alike she is a handy plaything.

But Osen had a toy, too: a paper airplane, as thin, as sharp-pointed as a spear.

> *One, a white star*
> *Two, a red star . . .*

In the mist she sings, and dreams: the reason she flies her paper airplane, the hatred that in her burns for human beings.

Osen, whose body is ageless, steps lightly over the grass, reaches the mere where the enfeebled old cast

themselves away to die. The paper airplane flies on against
the mist before her. No one knows what keeps the plane
flying so long. Once Osen lets go of it, the "airplane" flies
on seemingly forever. That's all there is to it. . . .

A madwoman, is Osen, going about naked in summer,
and in the winter wearing only one thin robe.

2

There is a traditional song that the village children
sang while playing ball, of which I vaguely recall one part:

> *I'll wait if it flies,*
> *if it doesn't I won't—*
> *I alone will keep waiting here.*
> *I wonder if I'll ever climb*
> *those weed-grown stairs someday—*
> *One star far and two stars near . . .*

Naked in the summer, and in the winter she wears one thin
robe.

Most adults ignored the children who jeered at Osen,
but there were a few who scolded them.

"Shame on you! Stop it! You should *pity* poor Osen."

The children just backtalked, often redoubling their
jeers to the tune of a local rope-skipping song, or else
throwing catcalls back and forth.

"Hey, *Gen!* Ya fall in *love* with Osen? Ya *sleep* with her
last night?"

"Don't be an idiot!"

Even if adults reprimanded them like this, the kids
kept up exactly the same sort of raillery. After all, everyone
knew that last night, or the night before, or the night

before that, at least *one* of the village men made love to Osen.

Osen: She must have been close to her forties. Some villagers claimed she was much, *much* older than that, but one look at Osen put the lie to their claims: She was youthful freshness incarnate, her body that of a woman not even twenty.

Osen: community property, harlot to all who came for it, the butt of randy male superiority. Coming to know the secrets of her body was a kind of "rite of passage" for all the young men of the village.

Osen: the village idiot. This was the other reason why the villagers sheltered her.

Osen was the only daughter and survivor of the village's most ancient family. Among those who live deep in the mountains and still pay homage to the Wolf God, the status of a household was regarded as supremely important. That such an imbecile should be the sole survivor of so exalted a household gave everyone a limitless sense of superiority—Osen! Plaything for the village sports!

Her house stood on a knoll, from where you could look down on Endworld Mere. Perhaps it's better to say where her house was *left*, rather than stood. At the bottom of the stone stairs leading up to her door, the openwork gate to her yard didn't know whether to fall down or not. Tiles were ready to drop from the gate roof, and tangled weeds and grass overgrew the ruins of the small room where long ago a servant would hold a brazier for the gatekeeper's warmth in winter.

A step inside the gate and the stone stairs leading up were choked with moss and weeds. The curious thing was, the center of the stairway had not been worn down; rather, both sides were. Nobody ever walked in the middle, say the old stories. According to the oldest man in the village,

on New Year's Eve they used to welcome in the new year
and send off the old with a Shinto ritual, and in one line of
the chant there was a passage about a Gate protected by the
Center of a Stone Stairway built by a forgotten Brother-
hood; and since no one knew the meaning of that, the old
man said, people felt it best to avoid the center of *this* stone
stairway whenever they passed up or down it.

The stairway climbed a short way beyond Osen's
house to where the ground flattened and widened out and
was covered with a profusion of black stones. An old
crumbling well with a collapsing roof propped up by four
posts was there. Sunk into the summit of this hill, one of
the highest points in the valley, the well had never gone
dry: Fathoms of water always filled it. If any high mountains had been massed nearby this would have explained
such vast quantities of water; but there were no such
mountains, and this well defied physical law. Sinner's
Hole, they called it. When the men were finished with
Osen they came to this wellside to wash.

Once when a shrill group of crackling old women
gathered at the well to hold yearly memorial services and
pray to the Wolf God, one of them was suddenly stricken
with a divination and proclaimed that if Osen were soaked
in the well, her madness would abate. This cheered up
those who envied Osen's great beauty, so on that day
twelve years ago poor Osen was stripped to the raw before
the eyes of the assembled women and dunked into the
winter-frigid well water. An hour later, her body blushed a
livid purple, Osen fainted and was finally hauled out. Sadly
her idiocy was not cured. Story has in that the old crone
who blurted the augury was drunk on the millet wine being
served at the memorial service, and that afterward she fell
into Endworld Mere and drowned. Because of the wine?

From then on, once someone undressed her, Osen

stayed that way. If someone draped a robe over her, she kept it on. Since someone undressed her nearly every night and left her as she was in the morning, Osen most often went around naked.

Beautiful as the men might find Osen's body, others thought it best to keep the children from seeing her. Therefore, each morning a village woman came around to see that she was dressed. Osen stayed stone-still when being dressed, though sometimes she smiled happily. She went on singing her songs—

> *Folding one,* dah-dum
> *fold a second one,* tah-tum
> *a third one fold,* tra-lah!
> *Fly on, I say fly!*
> *Fly ever on to my star!*

—folding her paper airplanes while she murmured and sang. And one day soon, to the stunned amazement of the villagers and eventual focus of their great uproar, Osen's stomach began growing larger.

No one had ever stopped to think that Osen might someday be gotten with child.

The village hens got together and clucked about it, fumbling in their brains for hours to find someway to keep Osen from having the child. Finally they moved en masse to the ramshackle house where Osen lived her isolated life, and they confronted her with their will.

The idiot Osen, however, shocked everyone when for the first time in living memory she explicitly stated her *own* will: She would have this baby.

"Osen! No arguments. We're taking you to the city, and you'll see a doctor."

"Don't be *ridi*culous, Osen. Why, you couldn't raise it if you had it. The poor thing would lead a p*athet*ic life!"

Large tears welled in Osen's eyes and spilled down her cheeks. None of the village women had ever seen Osen weep before.

"Osen . . . baby . . . I *want it born*. . . ." said Osen. She held her swollen stomach, and the tears kept streaming down her face.

How high in spirit and firm in resolve they had come here to drag Osen away! Why it all evaporated so swiftly they would never know. Captured now by the pathos, they, too, could only weep.

Osen soon dried her tears, and began folding a paper airplane.

"Plane, plane, fly off!" she cried. "Fly off to my father's home!"

The women exchanged glances. Might having a baby put an end to Osen's madness?

And then the paper airplane left Osen's hand. It flew from the parlor and out into the garden, and then came back again. When Osen stood up the airplane circled once around her and flew again into the yard. Osen followed it, singing as she gingerly stepped down the stone stairs, and her figure disappeared in the direction of the bamboo grove.

One old crone, with a gloomy, crestfallen face, took up a sheet of the paper and folded it; but when she gave the plane a toss it dipped, fell to the polished planking of the open-air hallway.

"Why does *Osen's* fly so well?" she grumbled.

Another slightly younger old woman said with a sage nod and her best knowing look, "Even a stupid idiot can do *some* things well, you know."

3

First month—red snapper!
hitotsuki—tai
Second month—then it's shells!
futatsuki—kai
Third, we have reserve, and
mittsu—enryōde
Fourth—shall we offer shelter?
yottsu—tomeru ka
If we offer shelter, well then,
tomereba itcho
Shall we fold up Sixth Day?
itsuyo kasanete muika
Sixth Day's star was seen—
muika no hoshi wa mieta
Seventh Day's star was too!
nanatsu no hoshi mo mieta
Eighth—a chalet daughter
yattsu yamaga no musume
Ninth—left crying in her longing
kokonotsu koishiku naitesoro
Tenth at last she settled in the small chalet!
tōto yamaga in sumitsukisoro
—*Rope-skipping song*

Osen kept flying her airplanes, the village men kept
up their nightly visits to her bower, the village women
never ceased their fretting over her delivery . . . and one
moonlit night a village lad came running down her stone
stairs yelling: "She's *hav*ing it! Osen's baby's on the way!"

A boy was born and they named him Emon. When he
was nearly named Tomo—"common"—because Osen was

passed round and round among the village men, the old midwife quickly intervened.

"As the baby was comin out, Osen cried '*ei-mon*,'" the old woman reported. "That's what she said. I wonder what she meant."

"Emon. Hmmm . . ." said one of the other women gathered there.

"Well, try asking."

Addressing the new mother, the midwife said, "Osen, which do you prefer as a name for the baby—Tomo, or Emon?"

"*Emon*," Osen answered clearly.

"That's better, it's related to Osen's entry gate," said an old woman who had memorized the chants for the Year End Rites.

"How do you mean?" a fourth woman said.

"Emon means *ei-mon*, the Guardian Gates," said the old woman. "I've heard that in the old days the New Year's Eve rituals were recited only here, at Osen's house. *Ei-mon* is part of the indecipherable lines . . . let's see . . . ah, yes, 'You must go up the center of Heaven's Stairs, the stone stairs protected by *Ei-mon*, Emon's Gate.'"

At this a fifth woman nodded.

"Yes, that's right," she said, adding, "It's also in one of the songs we sing at the New Year's Eve Festival. Here . . . 'Emon came and died—Emon came and died—Wherever did he come from?—He came from a far-off land—Drink, eat, get high on the wine—You'll think you're flying in the sky . . .'"

"Hmmm, I see now," said the fourth woman. "I was thinking of the *emon* cloth one wears when they die. But a man named Emon came and died? And protects the gate? I wonder what it all means. . . ."

The women took pity on Osen's child and everyone resolved to lend a hand in raising him. But . . . Emon never responded to it: He had given only that first vigorous cry of the newborn, then remained silent, and would stay so for a long time to come.

"Ah, what a shame," one woman said. "I expect the poor deaf-mute's been cursed by the Wolf God. What else for the child of an idiot?"

"We said she shouldn't have it," another replied with a nod.

Indifferent to the sympathy of these women, Osen crooned a lullaby.

> *Escaped with Emon, who doesn't know,*
> *flow, flow . . .*

"Why it's a *Heaven Song*," one of the women said suddenly. "She just changed the name at the beginning to Emon."

Moved to tears by the madwoman's lullaby, the women spontaneously began to sing along.

> *Escaped with Emon, who doesn't know,*
> shiranu Emon to nigesōro
> *flow, flow, and grow old*
> nagare nagarete oisōro
> *all hopes dashed in this mountainous land.*
> kono yama no chide kitai mo koware
> *No fuel for the Pilgrim's fires—*
> abura mo nakute kōchū shimoyake
> *no swaying Heaven's Way.*
> seikankōkō obekkanashi
> *Emon has died, alone so alone,*
> Emon shinimoshi hitori sabishiku

wept in longing for his distant home.
  furusato koishi to nakisōro

Everyone so pitied Emon, but as he grew he in no way acknowledged their gestures of concern, and because of this everyone came to think the mother's madness circulated in her silent child's blood.

Not so. When he was awake Emon could hear everyone's voices, though they weren't voices in the usual sense. He heard them in his head. "Voice" is a vibration passing through the air, sound spoken with a will. What Emon heard was always accompanied by *shapes*. When someone uttered the word "mountain" the syllables *moun-tain* resounded in the air; the shape projected into Emon's mind with the word would differ depending on who spoke it, but always the hazy mirage of a mountain would appear. Listen as you will to the words *Go to the mountain,* it is possible to distinguish five syllables. But in young Emon's case, overlapping the sound waves he could sense some one thing, a stirring, a *motion* that swept into a dim, mountainous shape.

For the tabula rasa mind of the infant this is an enormous burden. Emon's tiny head was always filled with pain and tremendous commotion. The minds and voices of the people around him tangled like kaleidoscopic shapes, scattering through his head like voices and images on the screen of a continuously jammed television set. It's a miracle Emon did *not* go mad.

No one knew Emon had this ability, and men kept calling on Osen as usual. In his mind Emon soon began walking with tottering, tentative steps: Along with, oh, say, Sakuzo's or Jimbei's shadowy thoughts would come crystal-clear images, and with them came meanings far beyond those attached to the spoken words.

"Hey there, Emon," they might say. "If you go out and play I'll give you some candy." Or they would say something like: "A *big whale* just came swimming up the river, Emon!"

But Emon's mind was an unseen mirror reflecting what these men were really thinking. It differed only slightly with each man.

And then one day when he was five years old, Emon suddenly spoke to a village woman.

"Why does everyone want to sleep with Osen?" he asked.

Osen, he said; not *Mother*. Perhaps because he kept seeing things through the villagers' minds, Emon was unable to know Osen as anything more than just a woman.

"E-emon-boy, you can *talk*?" the woman replied, eyes wide with surprise.

Shocking. Once Emon's power of speech was known, they couldn't have the poor boy living in the same house with that common whore Osen. . . . So the men hastily convened a general meeting, and it was concluded that Emon should be placed in the care of "the General Store"—the only store in the village.

This automatically meant that Emon must mix with the children's society; but as he knew so many words and their meanings at the same time, the other children were little more than dolts in comparison and could never really be his playmates. And not to be forgotten: Since he was Osen's child the other boys and girls considered him unredeemably inferior, and held him in the utmost contempt. So it was that reading books and other people's minds soon became Emon's only pleasure.

4

I once spoke to Osen while gazing into her beautiful
clear eyes.

"You're pretending," I told her. "You're crazy like a
fox, right?"

Instead of answering, Osen sang a song, the one she
always sang when she flew the paper airplanes, the ballad
of a madwoman:

> *Escaped with Emon, who doesn't know,*
> *flow, flow, and grow old . . .*

The "Heaven Song," of course. Now, if I substitute
some words based on the theory I'm trying to develop,
why, what it suggests becomes something far grander:

> *Shilan and Emon fled together,*
> Shiranu to Emon to nigesōro
> *Fly, fly, and they crashed,*
> nagare, nagarete ochisōro
> *the ship's hull dashed in this mountainous land.*
> kono yama no chide kitai mo koware
> *No fuel—the star maps have burned,*
> abura mo nakute kōchūzu mo yake
> *interstellar navigation is not possible.*
> seikankōkō obotsukanashi
> *Emon has died, alone so alone,*
> *Wept in longing for his distant home.*

The last two lines of this song remain the same as in
the version recorded earlier, but all of the preceding lines
have subtly changed. For example: In line one, *shiranu*

would normally be taken to mean "doesn't know," but in my reinterpretation it is now seen as the Japanization of a similar-sounding alien name—*Shilan*. In the second line, I am supposing that *oisōro* (meaning "grow old") is a corruption of the word *ochisōro* (meaning "fall" or "crash"); and I am further assuming that *kōchū shimoyake* ("Pilgrim's fires") in line four is a corruption of *kōchūzu mo yake* ("star charts also burned"). In lines three, four, and five, three words have double meanings:

> *kitai* = hope/ship's hull
> *kōchū* = pilgrim/space flight
> *seikankōkō* = heavenly way/interstellar navigation

In the above manner, line three changes its meaning from "all hopes dashed in this mountainous land" to "the ship's hull dashed in this mountainous land," and so forth.

There is more of this sort of thing. . . .

Once a week an ancient truck rattled and wheezed up the steep mountain roads on the forty-kilometer run between the village and the town far below, bearing a load of rice sent up by the prefectural government's wartime Office of Food Rationing. This truck was the village's only physical contact with the outside world. The truck always parked in front of the General Store.

Next door to the store was a small lodging house where the young men and women of the village always congregated. The master of the house was Old Lady Také, a huge figure of a woman, swarthy-skinned and well into her sixties, who was rumored to have once plied her trade in the pleasure quarters of a distant metropolis. She welcomed all the young people to her lodge.

On summer evenings the place was usually a hive of

chatter and activity. Even small children managed for a
short time to mingle in the company of their youthful
elders, dangling their legs from the edge of the open-air
hallway. Rope-skipping and the bouncing of balls passed
with the dusking day, and the generations changed. Small
children were shooed home and girls aged from twelve or
thirteen to widows of thirty-five or thirty-six began arriving, hiding in the pooling shadows. They all came seeking
the night's promise of excitement and pleasure.

It was an unwritten law that married men and women
stay away from the lodge, though the nature of their
children's night-play was an open secret. And how marvel-
ously different this play was from the play in larger towns
and cities: The people who gathered at Old Lady Také's
lodge doused the lights and immediately explored each
other's bodies. This, it must be said, was the only leisure
activity they had. In the mountains, where you seldom find
other diversions, this is the only amusement. The muffled
laughter of young girls as hands slipped beneath their
sweat-damped robes, their coy resistance. . . . And the
heady fragrance that soon filled the room drew everyone on
to higher delights.

Occasionally one of the local wags would amble by the
lodge, and from a safe distance flash a startling light on the
activities. Girls squealed, clutching frantically at their
bodies, draping their drenched clothes over their thighs. In
order to salvage this particular night's mood, someone
asked in a loud voice:

"Say, Osato, your son's gonna be coming around here
any day now, isn't he?"

"*What?*" said the widow.

"Yeah—he finally made it. I think!"

"Ho!" she laughed. "Ho! You're being nasty, kid. He's
only twelve. . . ."

"Well, if he hasn't, he'll find out how to pretty soon," the voice continued. "So maybe you should ask Osen as soon as possible. . . . ?"

"Hmmm . . . You might be right. Maybe tomorrow. I could get him spruced up, take him over in his best kimono. . . ."

A young man's voice replying from deep within the room said, "Naw, you're too late, Osato."

"And just what is *that* supposed to mean?"

"For Gen-boy it's too late. He beat you to it. It's been a month already." Laughter. "His mother's the last to know!"

"But *he* never . . . Oh, that *boy*."

As ever, Emon was near them all and listened to their banter. And sometimes, as everyone moved in the dark, he searched their minds.

(There'll be trouble if she gets pregnant. . . .)

(Ohhh, *big*. It'll *hurt*. What should I do if I'm forced too far?)

(I wonder who took my boy to Osen's place? I *know* he didn't go alone. Yard work for that boy tomorrow, lots. I'll teach *him*. And I was waiting *so* patiently. . . .)

Emon's mind-reading powers intensified among them as he roved over their thoughts night after night. He could see so clearly into their thoughts that it was like focusing on bright scenes in a collage. He was therefore all the more puzzled by his mother, Osen. She was different. Didn't the thoughts of a human being exist in the mind of an idiot? The thoughts of the villagers were like clouds drifting in the blue sky, and what they thought was so transparent. But in Osen's mind thick white mist flowed always, hiding everything.

No words, no shapes, just emotion close to fear turning there. . . .

As Emon kept peering into the mist, he began to feel that Osen let the men take her so that she might escape her fear. Emon gave up the search for his mother's mind and returned to the days of his endless reading.

His prodigious appetite for books impressed the villagers.

"What a bookworm!" one of them remarked. "That kid's *crazy* about books."

"You're telling me," another said. "He read all ours, too. Imagine, from Osen, a kid who likes *books*."

"Wonder who taught him to read. . . ."

Visiting all the houses in the village, Emon would borrow books, and on the way he tried to piece together a picture of his mother's past by looking into everyone's minds. *Was Osen an Idiot from the time she was born?* he wanted to know. But no one knew about Osen in any detail, and the only thoughts men entertained were for her beautiful face and body. Her body, perhaps ageless because of her imbecility, was a strangely narcotic necessity for the men.

A plaything for all the men of the village, was Osen, even for the youngest: for all who wished to know her body. Their dark lust Emon could not understand, but this emotion seemed to be all that kept the people living and moving in this lonesome place—a power that kept the village from splitting asunder.

Osen—madwoman, whore: She seized the men, and kept them from deserting the village for the enchantments of far-off cities.

5

A memory from when I was stationed in the village: In front of Old Lady's Také's Youth Lodge some children are skipping rope. In my thoughts I hear:

> *First month—red snapper!*
> hitotsuki—tai
> *Second month—then it's shells!*
> futatsuki—kai
> *Third, we have reserve, and*
> mittsu—enryōde
> *Fourth—shall we offer shelter?*
> yottsu—tomeru ka

The rope-skipping song I recorded earlier in this tale. A little more theory: With only a shift in syllabic division the song now seems to mean:

| *hitotsu* | *kitai* |
| (one) | (ship's hull) |

| *futatsu* | *kikai* |
| (two) | (machines) |

and with but a single change of consonants we have:

| *mittsu* | *nenryōde* |
| (three) | (fuel) |

Almost like a checklist . . .

Eventually the day came when Emon entered school. He was given a new uniform and school bag, purchased with money from the village Confraternity of Heaven Special Fund, which had been created long ago to provide for Osen's house and living. Emon went happily to the Extension School, which was at the far end of the village. There, in the school's library, he could read to his heart's content.

Miss Yoshimura, the schoolteacher, was an ugly woman, long years past thirty, who had given up all hope of marriage almost from the time she was old enough to seriously consider it. Skinny as a withered sapling and gifted with a face that couldn't have been funnier, yet she was a kindhearted soul, and of all those in the village she had the richest imagination and most fascinating mind. Having read so many books, she knew about much more than anyone else; and the plots of the uncountable stories she had read and remembered! They merged like twisting roots in her imagination, until they seemed to be the real world, and "reality" a dream. Most important, though, where everyone else never let Emon forget his inferiority, only Miss Yoshimura cared about him as equal to the others. Emon readily became attached to her, and was with her from morning until evening.

One day the old master of the General Store came to Miss Yoshimura.

"Ma'am," he began, "Emon's smart as a whip, but there's gonna be trouble if he becomes, you know, grows up too early."

"Ahm, oh, well . . . " Miss Yoshimura said, flustered.

"Since he's got Osen's blood and what not," the old man went on assuringly, "and watches the youngsters get together at Old Lady Také's place . . . well, if he gets like Osen, there'll be trouble. Some girl'll wind up gettin' stuffed by him, sure enough."

Embarrassed, Miss Yoshimura said, "Well, what do you think it best to do then?"

"Now as to that, we was thinkin' since he dotes on you so, it might be better for him to stay at your lodgin' house. Of course, the Confraternity Fund'll pay all his board."

"All right, I don't mind at all," said Miss Yoshimura,

perhaps a bit too quickly. "Of course, only if he *wants* to do
it. . . . How I *do* pity the poor child. . . ."

And in her thoughts an imaginary future flashed into
existence, pulsing with hope—*no I could never marry but
now I have a child whom I will raise as my own and days
will come when we hesitate to bathe together oh Emon yes
I'll be with you as you grow to manhood*—Her face
reddened at her thoughts.

Emon came to live in her house, then, and happy days
and months passed. Most happily, the other children
ceased to make so much fun of him. And the men never
came around to sleep with Miss Yoshimura as they did with
Osen.

She avoided all men. Her mind shrieked rejection,
that all men were nothing more than filthy beasts. Emon
quite agreed. But what went on in her mind?

As much as she must hate and avoid men, Miss
Yoshimura's thoughts were as burdened as any other's by a
dark spinning shadow of lust, and come the night it would
often explode, like furnace-hot winds out of hell.

Squeezing little Emon and tasting pain like strange
bitter wine, Miss Yoshimura would curl up tightly on the
floor with sharp, stifled gasps. The entangled bodies of men
and women floated hugely through her thoughts, and while
she tried to drive them away with one part of her mind,
another part reached greedily for something else, grabbed,
embraced, and caressed. Every word she knew related to
sex melted throughout her mind.

Miss Yoshimura always sighed long and sadly, and
delirious voices chuckled softly in her mind.

(*Oh, this will never do. . . .*)

Denouements like this were quickly undone, usurped
by their opposites, images flocking in her head, expanding
like balloons filled with galaxies of sex words that flew to

Osen's house. Miss Yoshimura fantasized herself as Osen, and grew sultry holding one of Osen's lovers. Then the lines of her dream converged on Old Lady Také's lodge, and she cried out desperately in the darkness:

"I'm a woman!"

Male and female shapes moved in the night around her. . . .

She returned to her room, where moonlight came in shining against her body. She moaned and hugged Emon fiercely.

"*Sensei,* you're killing me!"

At the sound of Emon's voice Miss Yoshimura momentarily regained herself—only to tumble yet again into the world of her fantasies.

(Emon, Emon, why don't you grow up. . . ?)

Conviction grew in Emon's mind as the days turned: In everyone's heart, including his dear *sensei*'s, there lurked this ugly thing, this abnormal desire to possess another's body. *Why?* Emon did not realize that he saw only what he wished to see.

Everyone's desire. From desire are children born. I already know that. But who's my father?

He kept up his watch on the villager's minds, that he might unravel that mystery, and he continued to gather what scrapes of knowledge that were remaining about his mother. More and more it appeared that she had escaped into her mad world to flee something unspeakably horrible.

In the mind of the General Store's proprietor he found this: (Osen's house . . . People say it was a ghost house in the old days, and then Osen was always cryin'. No, come to think about it, weren't it her mother? *Her* grandfather was killed or passed on. That's why she went crazy. . . .)

Old Lady Také's thoughts once whispered:

(My dead grandmother used to say that they were

hiding some crazy foreign man there, and he abused Osen, so they killed him, or something like that. . . .)

And the murmuring thoughts of Toku the woodcutter gave forth a startling image.

(Granddad saw it. Osen's house was full of blood and everyone was dead, murdered. That household was crazy for generations, anyway. Osen's father—or was it her brother?—was terrible insane. Ah' in the middle a' all them hacked bodies, Osen was playing with a ball.)

Old Genji knew part of the story, too:

(Heard tell it was a *long* time ago on the hill where the house is that the fiery column fell from the sky. Since around then all the beautiful girls were born in that family, generation after generation, an' couldn't one of 'em speak. That's the legend.)

Long ago, in days forgotten, something terrible happened. Osen alone of the family survived and went mad, and became the village harlot. This was all that was clear to Emon.

6

They say that time weathers memory away: In truth the weight of years bears down on memory, compressing it into hard, jewel-like clarity. A mystery slept in that village, and sleeps there still. Over the years my thoughts have annealed around these puzzling events, but the mystery will remain forever uncovered—unless I go there and investigate in earnest.

I have tried to return many times. A year ago I came to within fifty kilometers of the village and then, for no rational reason I can summon up, I turned aside, went to another, more *amenable* place. Before embarking on these journeys I am always overcome by an unshakable reluctance, almost as if I were under a hypnotic compulsion to stay clear of the place.

Another curious fact:

In all the time I was stationed there, I recall no else from the "outside" ever staying in the village more than a few hours; and according to the villagers I was the first outsider to be seen at all in ten years. The only villagers who had lived outside those isolated reaches were Old Lady Také and Miss Yoshimura, who left to attend Teacher's College.

If going there I actually managed to come near the village proper, unless the military backed me I feel certain the locals would somehow block my return.

Is there something, some power at work that governs these affairs?

Such a power would have a long reach and strong, to the effect that this village of fewer than two hundred people may exist outside the administration of the Japanese government. I say this because during the Pacific War no man from that village was ever inducted into the Armed Forces.

And who might wield such power? Who mesmerized everyone? Old Lady Také, or the Teacher? And if both of them left the village under another's direction, who then is the person central to the mystery?

The madwoman, Osen?

When summer evenings come, my memories are crowded with the numerous songs the village children sang. It was so queer that everything about those songs was at complete variance with the historical roots that those villagers claimed to have: That the village had been founded centuries earlier by fugitive retainers deserting the Heike Family during their final wars with the Genji in the Heian Period, and that since that time no one had left the village. Yet none of the old stories lingering there were of Heike legends. It is almost as if the village slept in the cradle of its terraced fields, an island in the stream of history, divorced from the world.

Is something still hidden beneath the stone stairs leading up to Osen's house? "Unknown Emon" gave up in despair and abandoned *some*thing there. A pump to send water up to the well at Sinner's Hole, or something hinted at in the children's handball song:

> *I wonder if I'll ever climb*
> *those weed-grown stairs someday?*
> *One—a stone stairway in the sky*
> *Two—if it doesn't fly,*
> *if it never flies open* . . .

When the day of flight comes, will the stairs open? Or must you open them in order to fly?—Questions, questions: It may be that the mystery of "unknown Emon" will sleep forever in that place.

And what became of Osen's child?

After a time Emon once again attempted what he long ago had given up on—a search of his mother's mind. The strange white mist shrouding Osen's thoughts was as thick as ever.

(Begone!)

Emon's thoughts thundered at the mist in a shock wave of telepathic power.

Perhaps the sending of a psychic command and the discharge of its meaning in the receiver's mind can be expressed in terms of physics, vectors of force; then again, it may just be that Emon's telepathic control had improved, and he was far more adept at plucking meaning out of confused backgrounds. Whatever: With his command, the mist in Osen's mind parted as if blown aside by a wind, Emon peered within for the first time.

Her mind was like immensities of sky. Emon dipped quickly in and out many times, snatching at the fragmented leavings of his mother's past. The quantity was small, with no connecting threads of history: everything scenes in a shattered mosaic.

There was only one coherent vision among it all: A vast machine—or a building—was disintegrating around her, and a mixture of terrible pain and pleasure blazed from her as she was held in a man's embrace.

And that was *odd:* that out of all her many encounters with all the men of the village, only this one experience had been so powerful as to burn itself indelibly into her memory.

The age and face of this man were unclear. His image was like seaweed undulating in currents at the bottom of the sea. The event had occurred on a night when the moon or some other light was shining, for his body was bathed in a glittering blue radiance. All the other men Osen had known, lost forever in the white mist that filled her mind and robbed her will, and only *this* man whom Emon had never seen existed with a force of will and fervency. Joy flooded from the memory, and with it great sorrow.

Why this should be was beyond Emon's understanding.

A vague thought stirred: *This man Osen is remembering is my father. . . .*

While Emon poked tirelessly through the flotsam in the minds of his mother and the villagers, Miss Yoshimura played in a fantasy world where her curiosity focused always on Osen. It was now customary for her to hold Emon at night as they lay down to sleep, and one night her heart was so swollen with the desire to be Osen and lay with any man that it seemed ready to burst.

How could she know that Emon understood her every thought?

How could anyone realize the terrible wealth of pure *fact* that Emon had amassed about their hidden lives?

But his constant buffeting in this storm of venery took its awful toll. Excluding the smallest of children, Emon was of the unswayable opinion that all the villagers were obscene beyond the powers of any description. Especially Osen and himself—they were the worst offenders. Through the minds of the men he was constantly privy to Osen's ceaseless, wanton rut, and the pain that he was Osen's child was heavy upon him. Ever she bared her body to the men, and . . .

Emon hated her. He hated the men who came to her, and in his superlative nine-year-old mind this wretched emotion was transformed into a seething hatred for all the human race.

It was on one of his infrequent visits to his mother that he at last vented his anger, and struck an approaching man with a hurled stone.

"Drop dead, you little bastard!" the man raged. "Don't go makin' any trouble, if you know what's good for you. Who d'ya think's keepin' you *alive!*"

Emon returned to the parlor after the man left and gazed at his silent mother's dazzling, naked body. He shook with unconcealed fury.

(I want to *kill* him! I *will* kill him! *Everybody!*)

Osen reached out to him then.

"My son, try to love them," she murmured. "You *must*, if you are to live. . . ."

Stunned, Emon fell into her arms and clung to her.

For the first time in his life he wept, unable to control the flow of tears.

Moments later Osen ended it all by releasing him and standing aimlessly, and that is when Emon began to suspect—to hope!—that her madness might only be a consummate impersonation. But it may have only been one clear moment shining through the chaos. There was no sign that the madness roiling Osen's brain had in the least abated.

Emon little cared to think deeply about the meaning of Osen's words, and his hatred toward the human race still filled his heart. But now he visited his mother far more often. It was during one of these visits, as he sat on the porch beside Osen some days or weeks later, that Emon *heard* a strange voice.

The voice did not come as sound in the air, or as a voice reaching into his mind with shapes and contexts. It was a *calling*, and it was for Emon alone—a tautness to drag him to its source, a thrown rope pulling. Unusually garbed in a neat, plain cotton robe, Osen was staring down the long valley, her mind empty as always.

"Who is it?" Emon called.

Osen turned her head to watch Emon as he scrambled to his feet and shouted the question. The vacuous expression on her face suddenly blanched, frozen for an instant in a look of dread.

"*Where are you!*" Emon shouted.

As if pulled up by Emon's voice, Osen got slowly to her feet and pointed to the mountains massed on the horizon.

"It's over there," she said. "That way . . ."

Emon hardly glanced at her as he started down the stone stairs, and then he was gone. He didn't even try to look back.

Time froze in yellow sunlight for the madwoman, and then melted again. Osen wandered blindly about, racked with sobs, at some point arriving at the small waterwheel shack that housed the village millstone. The violence of her weeping resounded against the boards. She may have lost her capacity for thought, but she could still feel the agony of this final parting from her only child.

One of the villagers, catching sight of her trembling figure as he passed by, approached her with a broad grin, reached for her body with calloused hands.

"Now, now, don't cry, Osen," he said. "Here, you'll feel lots better. . . ."

The look she fixed him with was so hard and venom-filled, the first of its like he had ever seen from her. For a moment he felt a faint rousing of fear shake his heart, then slapped his work clothes with gusto and laughed at his own stupidity.

"Now what in hell . . ." And cursing Osen, he grabbed to force her to the grassy earth.

Osen slapped his hands away.

"Human *filth!*" she shouted clearly, commandingly. Her words echoed and re-echoed in the stony hollows around the water mill: "Be gone and *die!*"

As Emon hurried far off down the road, the witless villager walked placidly into Endworld Mere, a dreamy look transfixing his face as he sank unknown beneath the dark and secret waters.

In the bamboo grove white mist danced again on the back of the air, and a white naked woman-figure ran lightly, lightly, chasing a paper airplane that flew on and on forever.

At the *Sai no Kawara*, the earthly shore where children come to bewail the passing of those who have crossed over the Great Waters, there is a weather-beaten sign of wood inscribed with characters that can only be spottily read:

> It seems so easy to wait one thousand—nay, ten thousand years . . . driven mad with longing for the Star of my native home . . .

A READING LIST OF JAPANESE SCIENCE FICTION IN ENGLISH

Note: KEL = Kodansha English Library

ABE, Kobo
The Ark Sakura. New York: Knopf, 1988
Inter Ice Age 4. New York: Knopf, 1970

ARAI, Motoko
Green Requiem. Tokyo: KEL, 1984
A Ship to the Stars. Tokyo: KEL, 1984

HOSHI, Shinichi
   The Capricious Robot. Tokyo: KEL, 1986
   The Spiteful Planet and Other Stories. Tokyo: Japan
      Times, 1978
   There was a Knock. Tokyo: KEL, 1984

KOMATSU, Sakyo
   Japan Sinks. New York: Harper & Row, 1976

TAKACHIHO, Haruka
   The Great Adventures of Dirty Pair. Tokyo: KEL,
      1987

TSUTSUI, Yasutaka
   The African Bomb and Other Stories. Tokyo: KEL,
      1986